# PRAISE FOR
## OTH

GW00469778

"Sara Century writes with subtle intensity and care. In a genre often extreme, alien, and operatic, her horror stories drop us into the small center of our familiar, vulnerable human core and send ripples spreading outward, enlarging gradually to create a total emotional effect. *A Small Light...* is a book full of dark awakenings."

— JOE KOCH (*THE WINGSPAN OF SEVERED HANDS, CONVULSIVE*)

"Century's fiction packs the potency of a nightmare that haunts the mind long after one has woken. She weaves dark poetry out of her character's relation-ships and crafts imagery designed to unsettle and inspire awe in equal measure. These stories whisper in your ear in the dark of night, and you will find yourself welcoming their insidious omens with outstretched arms."

— BRENDAN VIDITO (*PORNOGRAPHY FOR THE END OF THE WORLD, NIGHTMARES IN ECSTACY*)

# A Small Light
## & Other Stories

## Sara Century

WEIRD
PUNK

# Contents

# Slipping But Not Falling

Jessica pushed the key into the ignition but didn't start the car, letting her head rest against the steering wheel. She spoke a string of curses into the night; all muttered under her breath so that they came out as a long, bumpy growl. The gas station was one of the only places open on the dark road off the highway at midnight, and she'd desperately needed to get out and stretch her legs. The wind kicked pieces of trash around under the fluorescent lights. Past the road, everything was just a black and gray blur. Clouds obscured even the stars. She muttered a second long, rambling curse, and after she ran out of air, she took a deep breath, then a deeper one, and for a moment, everything was still.

"Hey, lady!" A hand banged on her windshield, and she nearly jumped out of her skin. A teenager stood there, gazing at her with concerned eyes. The kid looked like they'd climbed out of a pile of dirty laundry, but their body language was harmless. After all, she was wearing yesterday's clothes, too. "My mom wants you to move. She needs to use the pump."

Jessica glared at the kid more harshly than she intended through bloodshot eyes. She looked around. There were multiple empty spots, but the angry woman in the car behind her had her heart set on this one. She sneered slightly back at the woman, annoyed at her child-ishness, but also felt a quick moment of sympathy for the kid. One look in their quietly pleading eyes, and she knew this kind of thing happened all the time.

Jessica gave a quick nod and obeyed, pulling ahead and away from the gas pump. She glanced in her rearview only to see the woman flipping her off and yelling as her child rejoined her in the car. "Good luck," Jessica breathed and paused by the parking lot's exit to take a long drink of coffee.

She'd been planning on driving further down the coast well into the dark hours, but her grasp on reality was getting fuzzier and fuzzier, and it seemed past time for her to get a room. Even as she gulped coffee, she knew it wouldn't keep her awake much longer. She weighed her options. She wasn't on a schedule, yet she wanted to stay on the road. She feared that taking a moment to doubt her choices would open up space to regret them, and from there, she would inevitably be on the phone with Alice, begging for forgiveness, turning the car around, and driving all the way back home.

She felt compelled to keep moving, as if, when she stopped, Alice would catch up again. She'd left her phone in Seattle, and she didn't miss it, but not having it during the long distances between towns was just another thing that made her feel a little more exposed, a little less safe.

She hadn't missed the GPS, having chosen to simply follow the road signs that took her in the general direction of her sister's house outside of Miami. In the electrifying first hours of the trip, she'd known she would figure it out when she got there. Now, she felt like a dying battery.

The radio was off because it gave her anxiety to listen to it, so she heard the car pull up behind her despite its surprisingly quiet engine. A black muscle car with a large silver bird painted onto the hood, windows too dark to see the driver. Jolted awake, Jessica pulled out of the parking lot and towards the hotel across the highway. The car followed directly behind her for long enough to make her nervous, then the engine roared, and the car sped past her and vanished into the night. She laughed a brittle, alarmed laugh, then began worrying again as she crept at a snail's pace through the dimly lit parking lot.

She stopped in front of the hotel, which was admittedly beautiful, even in the dark. A white building with red roofs and doors and tall, thin windows overlooking the gray beach and the moody sea. Typically, it would be well out of her price range, but a hurried, anxious tallying of numbers and weighing the pros and cons in her mind told her that it wouldn't be so much more expensive than any other hotel along the way.

The radio suddenly jolted back on, filling the car with a wave of harsh static. She fumbled, spilling her coffee, and shut the car off. Another deep sigh and she got out, staggering slightly due to her full three days of driving and minimal exercise. She greedily drank another gulp of the black, slightly burnt liquid, achingly missing her espresso machine back home, and prepared herself to check in.

The front desk clerk was a woman of twenty-five or so, a good fifteen years younger than Jessica, with bleached hair and bright lipstick. Her textbooks were stacked up on each other on the counter. She seemed eager to get back to studying, and Jessica was happy to take her key and go on her way. She dragged her roller bag out of the trunk and pulled it behind her down the hall. The wheels made a gentle whirring noise, but the place was otherwise surprisingly quiet. She found her room—214, near a staircase, towards the end of a hall.

Jessica locked the door, deadbolted it, and made sure the windows were closed. She checked under the bed and in the closet to ensure she was completely alone, then fell onto the bed without taking her clothes off. She meant to get back up, but she struggled to stay awake. Slowly, she kicked her shoes off, squirmed out of her jacket and skirt, and pulled her quilt out of her bag and around her shoulders. She was hungry, but it didn't matter. She fell asleep with the lamp on the table still on.

Late in the night, she awoke to a couple arguing in the parking lot. She tried to ignore it, but it got worse, so she decided to look and see what was going on, pulling the curtain back a bit. A man and a woman stood out in front of the hotel on the sidewalk, between two potted shrubs. Beyond them, there were twenty or thirty parked cars. Maybe more, maybe less, Jessica couldn't tell. The couple was white, both likely in their forties, wearing crumpled jackets, her over a flowery dress, him over a button-up shirt and slacks. He seemed to be scolding her, and his stance was aggressive as she tried to calm him. They both seemed a bit drunk. Jessica looked around outside and noticed the black car with the silver bird on the hood was parked next to her own dented, dirty Camry. She frowned.

No sooner had she seen the car than did its headlights flash on, catching the couple in a beam of bright light. They both threw up their arms to shield their eyes, shouting a few words Jessica couldn't quite make out. They seemed just as surprised as she was to see that someone had been sitting in the car all along. It sat motionlessly, but the lights stayed on. The man hesitantly started towards the car, but the lights shut off right as he reached it. The driver's side door kicked open, and a woman stepped out.

Jessica watched her and felt that she must still be in a dream. The woman wore a wide-brimmed black hat that hid her face. Her red jacket, black skirt, and black gloves were impeccable, not a thread out of place. Long, silvery hair rustled in the cold wind. Unable to see her face, Jessica found herself focusing on the visual softness of her, the way a pale aura glowed around her, and her long, silvery hair rustled over her shoulders in the cold wind. Her walk seemed almost like a dance as she strode brazenly towards the man, who appeared to be angry at first but quickly went silent. The woman in the hat drifted towards the hotel and the situation visibly relaxed. The couple quietly got into their Subaru and drove away.

Jessica was uneasy at the thought of the woman in the hat in the hotel for reasons she couldn't quite understand. She wondered how she would get back to sleep now, but no sooner did she lay down than she was out again.

If she hadn't been so tired, she might have heard the

scraping of fingers underneath the door to her room. She might have listened to the jiggling handle.

Her dreams were tortured and cruel. Alice was there, refusing to listen, distorting her words, holding her wrists too hard, accusing her of everything under the sun, and like the sun, the fire of her words burned. When she woke up, she'd already been crying for a long time. She let out another sob, loud but not so loud, and covered her mouth with her hands, weeping into them.

It took a while to realize how late in the day it was. She looked at the clock, which read 3:24 PM. Her eyes darted to the window, and she nervously pulled the curtain open, inch by inch, suddenly afraid that there might not be anything behind it. She breathed a sigh of relief to see the world was indeed still there. The sun was drooping in the sky, hidden by gray storm clouds that had not yet come close enough to bring rain. But they were coming closer.

Jessica threw on her hoodie and ran downstairs, confirming that they had charged her for another night. She vaguely remembered a financial transaction she had not been quite awake for over the hotel phone, but her anxiety demanded that someone confirm this for her. Everything was buried under the pain of her dream about Alice. Often, everything else eclipsed by the ache of loving someone who had hurt her so much. Even now, when she was so, so far away.

Jessica ran out the front door towards the gas station as the first drops of rain began hitting the pavement. The store was busy, and the fluorescent lights were disorienting, but it was somehow calming to be around people doing relatively normal things. She wandered through the food and drink aisles and bought $30 worth of junk food and coffee drinks. The skies had opened up in the amount of time it took her to pay. She ran back across the parking lot and sat under the awning in front of the hotel and watched the rain until a man walked out and casually tried to join her. He introduced himself and tried to shake her hand, but she shook her head and stood to leave. She went back inside without a second thought as he stared after her.

By the time she was showered and resting on her bed, it was seven o'clock. She stared at the ceiling for a long time and felt like she might vomit, but it never happened. The food and drinks were shoved into the mini-fridge, untouched. In the blink of an eye, two more hours had passed. She drank a glass of water and ate a handful of almonds and half of an orange. Her body drifted from heavy despair to a light, almost hysterical thirst. Thirst for something that she couldn't reach. For the life with Alice that she had never truly had. An impossible need. A desire that could not be fulfilled, clawing inside her, begging her to do things she didn't want to do.

"You could just call her," she whispered, then sat up and stared at herself in the mirror for a long time. The week had worn on her. The lack of a complete meal for so long had worn on her. There were grayish-blue bags under her reddened eyes, and her wrinkles were more pronounced than ever before. Her skin was pale and paper-thin, taking on an almost translucent quality that made her look like she'd been sick for a long time. She'd cut her brown and gray hair short only a few days before leaving. Alice had hated it, but Jessica had known she would. She'd been quietly planning to leave even then and

pushed a few buttons here and there in hopes of insti-
gating a fight that would give her an excuse to go. The
war never came, but she'd left, anyway.

Realizing that she would very likely lose her mind
before the night was over if she just sat in her room, she
decided to go for a walk through the hotel. The rain
continued to thrum against the windows. Lightning
crashed and crackled over the volatile sea, but it was
barely audible through the thick walls and windows and
the whirring ice machines. She still had yet to see anyone
besides the desk clerks, and it was odd, but she supposed
that it was off-season, full of bad weather and a new flu
strain that was knocking people out for weeks at a time.
Her mind rationalized these things quickly away so it
could devote more time to wondering if she'd made the
right choice in leaving Alice.

The halls were long and empty, and while she did hear
mumbling now and again behind closed doors, there was
no one out and about. She scanned the beige, tan, maroon
wallpaper and carpet, likely explicitly chosen for its
soothing and inoffensive look. Fake plants sat in various
corners, covering up peeling wallpaper or a stain on the
mat. All hotels looked much the same to her, and the
sameness made her sigh with weary monotony. Would
she even be able to remember this place once she'd left?
She doubted it.

She might not remember these small details of the
heavy maroon curtains that had collected just a little too
much dust since their last cleaning, but she felt confident
she would remember the rain. It had seemed to have
followed her from the start of her voyage days before. It
had been raining when she bolted out the front door with

a couple of bags and drove away from Alice, and it had poured down on her car through most of her drive so far. So much so that she'd lost sight of the road several times, and her windows had fogged up and made it impossible to see. Even when she was safe in bed in her sister's spare room, she knew she would remember how the rain seemed to be pushing her and pulling her.

The halls were repeating themselves. She took the turns she thought would bring her back to the stairs but went in a loop. She tried again and again, and the same thing happened. Her heartbeat pulsed faster, and she was breathing more heavily. She followed the sign that said EXIT, and it took her to a dead end. Her pace quickened, but everything was repeating.

When she finally found the stairs, she was overjoyed and jogged down to the first floor. She dismissed the moment of terror when she'd felt alone in an endless maze and focused on her feet as she walked across the lobby, waving shortly to the clerk from the night before, who almost certainly did not recognize her at all. She waved politely back but didn't smile.

Jessica hadn't intended to find her way to the hotel bar, but once she stumbled upon it, she had difficulty justifying leaving without a drink. The place was nicer than she expected, with heavy wooden tables and forgiving lighting, and flattering mirrors lined up along the walls. Soft piano music played behind her as she strode to the counter. She recognized Hazel Scott's Relaxed Piano Moods and respected the choice.

The bartender was Japanese-American, dressed in classic server attire of a black button-up shirt, tie, slacks, apron, and shoes. They had short hair and an undercut, some piercings, and a few indecipherable tattoos poked out of the tops of their shirts and sleeves, just like Jessica's. Their sleeves were rolled up to the elbow, and their top button was undone, which gave them a rakish charm that made Jessica immediately want to befriend them. They were casually bantering with a couple while opening a bottle of wine and pouring each of them a glass. They glanced and smiled at Jessica to let her know that they were aware of her arrival. Jessica stared briefly at the menu, choosing to order a Bloody Mary instead of food, justifying the choice by reminding herself of the snacks in the mini-fridge. Anyway, it might take a few more days of anxiety-driven nausea before she could stomach a meal.

A hand set down a glass of water in front of Jessica, interrupting her reverie. "You get a second to look at the menu?" the server asked. "I'm pleased to inform you that you made it for happy hour; wines and wells are half off."

"Can you make a Bloody Mary without the worchester?"

"Yes, but is it because you're vegan? Because we have vegan Worchester. I just made some earlier today, in fact."

Jessica folded the menu and laid it down on the counter as if it had played an enormous role in her decision-making process. "That sounds great. Can I get it extra spicy?"

"Spicy drink for a spicy day," the server said, then laughed. "Sorry, I clopened last night, and today my coworker called in, so I feel like I've been here for...ever. I have no idea what I'm saying. But fortunately, I can make a Mary with my eyes closed."

"What's a clopen?" Jessica asked, absently squeezing a lemon slice into her water.

"When you close, then open? So I closed last night and had to be back in at ten in the morning. And now..."

"It's ten. You've been here for twelve hours?"

"Yes! Minus about eight hours of sleep, I've been here for about two days. But I'll be happy about it when I get my check next week."

Within the hour, Jessica had learned that the server's name was Jen, that they were a lifelong local of thirty-one years though their parents had fallen in love in Jessica's hometown of Seattle, that their mom and dad had divorced when they were a child but had remarried last year, that they had one much older brother who lived in Alabama, and that they used to live with their partner but that had ended some time ago. They were thinking about going to grad school. They were still upset about the last season of Game of Thrones. They didn't have a car because they lived less than a mile away, and everything else was within biking distance. Business was pretty slow, which gave them a lot of time to chat while Jen did their side work and occasionally tended to other customers. Jessica relished the chance to act like an average person with casual concerns in life again, and Jen was self-aware enough to notice her skirting around questions about herself. Jessica had a couple of beers after the Bloody and had finally ordered some fries when she felt herself starting to fade.

Halfway through a sentence, Jen tensed, and their voice trailed off. Jessica looked into the mirrors behind her to see what they had seen, amused by their reaction. "Who's thaaaaat?" she teased in a singsong voice, but inwardly she felt the same jolt of anxiety that Jen experienced. It was the woman from last night—the woman in the wide-brimmed hat.

"She'll say her name is Sasha," Jen said tensely, then quickly poured three shots and set them in front of the woman as she pulled up a chair. Jen said nothing, no word of greeting, did not look directly at her, and did not ask her to pay. The woman likewise did not look up or acknowledge them at all. Several moments passed before she took one of the shots, setting the empty glass back down in front of her, next to the other two. Some new customers came in, and Jen gravitated towards the other side of the bar, away from Jessica and the woman in the hat.

The woman slightly tilted the brim upward and looked at Jessica with a smile. Her eyes were the same shimmering, soft gray as her hair. She appeared to be about Jessica's age but well-rested and vibrant, whereas Jessica was exhausted and pained. "My name is Sasha."

An image of Alice flashed through her mind, a strange assortment of moments. Angry and happy. Violent and generous. She wondered how long it would be before she could talk to someone without feeling afraid Alice would be jealous. She shook off the hesitation and gave Sasha her name. They briefly clasped hands in a greeting, a gesture that was both antiquated and far too intimate. Sasha took her second shot and looked up at her again. She was smiling, but it gave Jessica a chill.

They began to talk casually about the weather, the beauty of the sea, the history of the area. Sasha was well-informed and had many stories, none of which were hers, all of which were fascinating. The man after whom the city was named had lost his family in a boating accident over a century before and had spent the rest of his life in the hotel, unable to bear returning home without them. The strange nautical history of the area, which included many triumphs and interesting local customs, but also much tragedy by way of capsized boats and promising young lives cut short and nameless, unidentified bodies washing up on the shore, flesh stripped from the bones by hungry fish, piece by piece by piece.

Jessica was so engaged by Sasha's stories, which were historical but which sounded a bit like episodes of the Twilight Zone, that she barely noticed Jen's sudden distance, nor did it occur to her that she was getting much drunker than she realized. She stood and excused herself under the pretense of smoking a cigarette, resolving to go buy a pack even though she'd quit years before. Sasha smiled like she was letting her in on a secret as she pulled a pack out of her pocket, holding them up. "I'll come with you." If she hadn't been drinking, she might have noticed Jen's alarmed gaze following them as they walked together out into the rain.

As they walked out through the double doors, Jessica was surprised to see how badly it was coming down. It was hard to see very far ahead, even in the well-lit parking lot. They smoked, and Sasha began throwing out some facts about the architecture, the man who had designed the hotel, the fact that his family continued to be active in local politics even now. Jessica listened, and chatted with her, and blew great puffs of smoke out into the air. She began to think about turning in for the night, but wanted to have a last drink.

Just as her mind had started to drift to images of her warm bed, something the other woman said stopped her in her tracks. She froze, turning to look at Sasha, but her head was tilted down, her hat covering her face.

"What did you say?" Jessica whispered.

"Alice needs you," Sasha said. "Go to her."

Jessica's blood ran cold though her heart was thumping hard and fast. "What do you know about Alice?" she whispered.

Sasha's hand raised, and she pointed out into the darkness, towards the sea. Jessica turned, her eyes following where Sasha had indicated and her stomach sank. Looking past the parked cars, across the street, across the beach, she could only see the vaguest outline of the water, but it was Alice's frantic voice calling her name.

"Jessica!"

It was Alice! Jessica gasped, and stumbled forward. Alice! In the water, her head vanishing beneath the ocean waves. Jessica turned back to Sasha, but she was gone, though her cigarette smoke still lingered. Where did she go? To get help? Jessica turned back to the water. The figure was barely visible, sticking out of the water and disappearing again. There wasn't time to wait.

"Alice!" Jessica began running, kicking her clothes and shoes off as she went, her heart in her throat. As she ran towards the shore, a thousand inconsistencies rushed through her mind. Why would Alice be here? How had she followed Jessica all this way? Why was she in the water? How did Sasha know her name? Yet, the image of her wife engulfed by the frothing black and blue waves overrode everything. She could only think of Alice in her weakest moments now, crying with her head in Jessica's lap, begging her never to leave while Jessica swore she never would.

When she reached the shore, she could only barely see Alice, but she could still hear her. Without hesitation, she leapt into the waves, swimming towards her love. Yet, that wasn't right either, was it? She wasn't her love, at all. She was someone who Jessica had fled.

"Jessica! Jessica!" Alice cried, her mouth filling with saltwater as her head was pulled under.

"I'm coming!" Jessica shouted, swimming as fast as she could against the water and the rain, but it was a struggle to stay afloat, at all. The water pushed her under, again and again. She squinted, trying to see through the waves.

What she thought had been Alice, it looked like there was something else, covered in glistening scales, glinting like an oil rainbow in a puddle of water, mouth open, sharp teeth chomping at the air.

"Alice?"

"Jessica! Jessica!"

Jessica's eyes scanned the area, no longer looking for Alice, but now considering her surroundings. Alice was just out of the mouth of the bay, hovering in the open water, neither coming closer or moving further away. If Jessica went further, the water would be deeper, and it would be a lot harder to get back to shore. Why wasn't Alice swimming towards her?

She looked around frantically, the rain beating down on her as the waves pulled her in. "Jessica!" It seemed to be coming from all directions at once. "Jessica!" No. It was coming from the sea.

Jessica let herself start drifting back towards the shore. The waves no longer pulling her under, but rather, pushing her back towards safety.

"Alice?"

There was no noise at all besides the rain and the waves crashing against each other. If Sasha had gone to get help, they had not come, and that also seemed wrong.

"Alice?" she whispered, struggling to keep her head above the surface of the freezing cold water.

Unbidden, she remembered the last time she'd seen Alice. The last time they'd eaten dinner together, which was not a night of arguing or of violence, but rather just a small, numbing evening that meant nothing in the larger scheme of things. How Alice had seemed to barely tolerate her, but neither of them had the energy to fully broach the subject. How she wondered if she'd come to hate Alice, as well. Not the fights, and the way none of her friends talked to her anymore, or the hesitancy in her sister's voice when she said it was fine to come but not to bother if she was just going to go back to her again. Just one night among a thousand that didn't matter but drove the final nail in a coffin that had been closing and popping back open for years.

She thought of that night, but, mostly, she thought of how Alice hated the water. She hated the rain. She'd have never come to the beach. She'd have never followed her here.

Something hit Jessica hard, enough to send her spinning up into the air. She smacked against the waves and nearly breathed in a lungful of saltwater as her body reeled from the shock of it. A shark? An orca? Or the strange, glistening, humanoid thing she'd thought she'd seen? She began swimming towards the shore. The next time she was hit, it knocked her out cold, and the last thing she remembered was falling into the black-hued water, no longer able to tell which was up or down, her lungs struggling to breathe air that was not there.

Jessica was found on the beach late in the dreary light of the following morning, half-drowned but already recovering. Police came, and she spent most of the day in the hospital, watching TV reports of the many people who had gone missing in town over the last few years as police and doctors scolded her about the dangers of swimming at night. She was ultimately discharged. The sun had come out a bit in the afternoon and was hanging low in the sky when she made it back to the hotel, but she was terrified of seeing the woman in the wide-brimmed hat again. She knew it'd be better to drive on.

She checked out quickly, without fanfare, throwing her bag into the backseat in the fading sun. She looked at the sky for a long moment, her hand over her eyes as a shield for the bright last moments of daylight. Jen came out the side door and waved.

"Jessica! I'm so glad to see you alive!"

"I'm glad I have a chance to say goodbye! Aren't you on the clock?"

"Taking a smoke break. All loaded up, then?" Jen smiled.

"Yes."

"Ah. Well, it was a pleasure to meet you. Sorry you almost died."

"Maybe our paths will cross again," Jessica said, meaning the comment somewhat flippantly until she heard Jen's heavy sigh. Jessica turned to look at them directly.

Jen's smile wavered, but didn't vanish. "I say this with love in my heart... I think it's better if they don't." They pulled a pack of cigarettes out of their shirt pocket and lit two, handing one over to Jessica. They both took long, evenly paced drags from their cigarettes, staring out at the sea.

"I... I left my wife," Jessica said, and saying the words aloud gave them a finality that she hadn't realized she needed. "She was... well, it was... bad. The woman from last night..."

Jen nodded. "You don't have to tell me. I can guess." They sighed, resolving to explain. "My ex that I told you about. We were together for a few years, but her shitty ex had been contacting her again, and... well, she went missing, and even now... well, everyone thinks it was him, but... listen, I know how this sounds, but that woman last night? That was my ex. It was her... but it wasn't her. Do you understand? It... had her face."

"You mean she... has amnesia, or something?"

"I mean it wasn't her. The way she dresses. The way she talks. It's... it's not Sasha. The last time I saw her... she was with a woman... in a wide-brimmed hat. Someone who..."

"Led her to the shore," Jessica finished for her when Jen's voice trailed away.

"And when I called out to her... to try and call her back inside... it was as if she couldn't hear me. And I went back in because I thought... she was... ignoring me... I..." They wiped their tears away, but new ones came. "She's considered a missing person. But I still see her. I had to move from my old apartment because she would appear outside, stopped in the middle of the sidewalk, or sitting in a tree, or standing on the roof... trying to get inside, but not... remembering how, or why... and whatever she is, I know she is not Sasha. She's not her. But I think she remembers Sasha's life, and she keeps revisiting her memories, but it's like... it's like she doesn't know quite what they mean..."

They stood there for a few more minutes, but Jen had to go back to work, and Jessica needed, more than anything, to watch this whole town vanish in her rearview mirror. She waved goodbye to Jen and walked back to her car. After turning on some music, she began to pull out of the parking lot.

At the mouth of the drive, she paused to take a drink of water, but her heart jumped into her throat when she realized that the black car with the bird on the hood was behind her once more. She stared with alarm in her rearview only a moment, then turned carefully out onto the road. She watched as the black car waited, then, slowly, when she was almost out of sight, how it turned the opposite direction and vanished into the night.

THE BLACK CAR drove down the coast, eventually arriving in the mansion on the beach that she had spent months nesting in. The sound of her heels clacking against the tile floors all the way from the door to her bedroom was the only noise to be heard. Everything was dark. She took a seat at her vanity, and reached a hand over to click on the lights. She glanced into the mirror, thinking of how she'd always loved these eyes.

Her hand wandered up towards her neck, and in no time, she was pulling off the face, and the eyes, the hair, and the lips all along with it. She placed the Sasha on a mannequin head, glancing at all the others, wondering who she might go out as tonight. After all, there were dozens of different faces around the room to choose from. Different identities for her to try on as she saw fit.

All she knew for certain is that she needed to expand her hunting grounds to ensure her lover would be fed. Her beautiful, rainbow-scaled counterpart, a creature of legend just like her, alone in the sea, waiting all night for a meal that hadn't come. Her lover, who fed on flesh, as she herself fed on memories. The Jessica from last night may have been more trouble than she was worth, but it was Sasha's own fault for returning to that hotel to begin with. There were plenty of public spaces around, no need for her to go back to that one. Except the strange affinity she felt for the person in black who worked behind the bar, there was nothing there. And perhaps that affinity had cost her too much. Jessica would have been a good feast for her and her love, and a new mask, too. She desperately wanted to retire Sasha and her stale attachment to the bartender. She wanted to trade in all these faces, all their ghosts, for something new.

She decided on one that she hadn't worn in some time, a Veronica. She would be a Veronica when she went out tonight, but for now, she simply wished to be herself, smooth unbroken skin where eyes, a nose, and a mouth would be, if she were human. If she were human...

She sat quietly, alone, head tilted towards the mirror, existing only in her own reflection, basking in the strange pull of distant memories that were both hers and not hers at all.

# THE LAST DAYS OF THE PLAGUE

IT WAS THE FIFTH DAY OF OCTOBER WHEN THE FIRST DROPS of blood fell from Therese's nose as she was only just rising out of bed that morning. We had heard of some deaths from an unknown illness, but Death back then seemed far away. Therese smiled at me and said it was nothing, and I agreed. I agreed, but inside, my heart began to race, and a terrible, aching emptiness took root inside my chest. Over time, this painful absence began to grow. Small at first, but getting bigger, like the drops of red against the sheet that day. Small at first, but consuming, until there was nothing left of what once was. I imagine that this is what death is like.

That was the beginning of the plague for me. The realization of it hit everyone in different ways, and at different times. Some accepted it immediately, believing that the brutal death that surrounded us was final, definitive proof that their cold and distant God was finally paying attention, finally punishing us for our sins. Some never accepted the plague's existence, bartering against fate up to the last moment, dragging the living along with them as far as they could go before entering the final abyss where none could follow.

For Therese, I believe it did not fully strike until weeks later, in the last moments of her life, as her body became too weak to move, and she watched me care for her through eyes that had become slits, her face skeletal and her hands cold.

It was early that morning when I had awakened only to see Death standing over her. At first, I could only see the cloak, dirty and torn, but slowly the face became clear to me. It was rotted away, missing teeth, leaning in over Therese's bluing lips. Breathing in her breath before it could reach her lungs. Therese was coughing, asphyxiating. I tried to stop Death from taking her, but getting close was impossible. The aura around Death is toxic, and it only leads to a void. There is nothing there. I could not grab hold.

Therese's eyes flew open, wide and afraid. She tried to flee only to stumble and collapse in a pile on the ground. I shrieked, and wept, but it didn't matter. Within minutes, my beloved Therese was gone. Death was not moved by my grief. Death did nothing but vanish away.

A charcoal gray thundercloud settled over me.

I saw Death twice more after that.

The first time, I was sitting in a tavern that had once been reserved only for men. Indeed, the bodies of many men were stacked just outside the door. I stepped over the dying proprietor on my way to take a drink from the tap. I drank as much as I was capable of drinking, and so I was drunk by the time I turned to see Death, crouching over the dying barkeep, a long tongue forked into either of the man's eyes, drinking as heavily as me.

I screamed, and threw my mug at Death, but there was nothing to do. I leapt over the bar and stumbled out into the streets. I climbed up to a rooftop and watched as large segments of the city burned, the smell of bodies rising up in a permanent miasma over us, seeping into the souls of all who walked here.

The second time, I had begun coughing blood into my hands, much the same as Therese had all those months before. The city and its people had been devastated, and despite the constant rain, the smell of corpses never fully washed away. I had long ago left our home and took up residence in a tower at the edge of town, attached to the church. By then, no one buried the bodies anymore. There were too many and none of us had the strength. The cemetery was underneath me. I watched it day and night and waited for Death to come once more.

Death was standing in the room with me long before I knew they were there. The last surviving priest was praying at the other side of the room. I coughed. He coughed. Death started towards me. I stood and walked to the other side of the room, suddenly determined to escape him. I put my hands on the priest's shoulders, and shoved him out the window.

Death stood still for only a moment. Perhaps my last-ditch attempt at diversion puzzled them, but not for long. Death walked after the priest, but also walked through me. I gasped, and screamed. A cold shadow settled in my heart. Ever since then, I don't feel anything, good or bad. I don't feel anything at all. Death did not take me, but the coughing never stopped, and I see ghosts all around me.

Death did not take me, but I have remained in Hell never-theless.

I looked down out of the window at the man, crushed on the ground, bleeding, his eyes wide open, staring at the sky. I left the tower, and then the town, and I have never gone back since.

We are in the last days of our plague, now. There are few of us left, and we've all done terrible things to survive. I pass people on the paths that were once roads and I wonder if they've all seen Death, too. We've all certainly seen the dead. At the edge of my vision, I still see Therese's ghost, hand outstretched, crying out. I only hear her calling my name in my dreams, but I can always see her. Her fingers are stretching out to me, straining against themselves, reaching, reaching, reaching, and finding nothing there.

# THE HOLLOW BONES

THE FIRST TIME I WENT TO THE HOUSE WITH ALL THE GREAT gray windows facing the sea, I commented on its loveliness. Wispy clouds laced themselves throughout the moody sky and the brackish ocean water sparkled in the muted light. Birds dotted the shoreline, small silhouettes against the horizon. Difficult to tell where the house ended and the ground beneath it began. Just another rock poking up out of the sea, made of brick and concrete and glass.

I wanted to wait outside, but Cin insisted it would be a while and urged me to come in with her. I stared at our distorted reflections in the windows while we talked, but I did not look at her directly. She could always convince me, but it's hard to say in hindsight if that was because she was exceptionally persuasive or if I was just bad at drawing boundaries. I suppose it doesn't matter now. Together, we got out of the car.

"It's nice!" I strained to speak loud enough to be heard over the wind and sea.

"Wait until you see inside."

I went to respond but mist filled my eyes and mouth, and my voice trailed away. Cin took my hand in hers and pulled it into her pocket, leading me up the walkway to the front door. I pulled back, always more worried than her about what people might think. It seems foolish now, but back then I was only out to a few friends; no one else. Cin had always been out as·long as I'd known her. I used to think it was because she had less to lose than I did, but now, after everything that happened, I think she just thought it was worth the risk.

Cin struggled to find the phone number she'd been given while I hopped up and down trying to stay warm in the harsh wind. The door swung open just as she pushed the key in the lock, and we were greeted by Susan Emery, the lady of the house. She greeted us pleasantly and ushered us in.

Of course, Cin had already told me all about Susan. She was in her late forties, with dark hair and blue eyes, and wore a simple, vertically striped, black and white dress. A crystal bird on a silver chain rested on her collar; a piece of jewelry that Cin absolutely adored. Her eyes kept falling back on it as we talked. I was distracted and couldn't keep my eyes off of the birds.

The birds. Once you walked past the small entryway, the birds were everywhere. Cin had been hired to help care for and clean after them a few weeks before. Susan and her husband Mark's relationship had grown strained in their attempts to stay on top of the dozens and dozens of exotic birds they had purchased together over the last decade of their marriage. From what Cin had told me, they wanted to focus more on their personal life, the art gallery they owned together, and maybe even plan a vacation. They had been tending to the menagerie of macaws and cockatiels and parakeets and more together for a long time, and even with so much constant interaction, they had lost touch with each other. According to the ad for the job, the couple had over a hundred birds in their home, and Susan had bragged that they had nearly five hundred thousand dollars invested in them. "Lots of famous people have bird collections," Cin had explained to me after taking the job. "They're like pets, I guess. But it's weird, don't you think? Keeping birds."

They didn't seem much like pets to me. They were loud and apprehensive, nervously shifting from one foot to the other and calling sharply to one another, or perhaps to us. The whole time we were there, Susan didn't even seem to notice them, but they certainly noticed her. Their interactions all centered around her in some way, and they would look at her when she spoke or when she made any kind of gesture with her hands. I almost immediately stopped listening to Cin and Susan's small talk, distracted by the birds and their strange response to their keeper.

There were just so many of them. I had never seen that many in the same place before, not even in a zoo. Some in cages, some out, all different colors and sizes. I couldn't stop thinking about the malice in the act of placing another living thing in a cage, but I wondered if we didn't all do it at least metaphorically. I stared into the eyes of birds and tried to imagine what I looked like to them. What a strange, terrible sort of life, with a small chain around your foot, binding you to the ground. Maybe they thought the same of us, sitting on an uncomfortable couch, enduring meaningless conversations. Their eyes glistened.

"Sweetie?" Cin's voice broke through my reverie. "Susan asked if you want a drink?"

"No! Sorry. No thank you."

"No? Are you sure?" Susan asked, flashing a strange smile. "We've got so much leftover booze from our New Year's Eve party, we might never get rid of it all. You might take some with you, at least?"

"I don't really drink," I said.

"I do, I'd love a drink," Cin smiled.

Susan noticed that I'd left a few damp footprints by the door, which she mentioned casually, then became anxious and stood to go clean them. "I'm a bit of a neat freak," she explained, rapidly leaving the room to tend to the mess. I said nothing, taking a long, even sip from my water bottle. Cin looked at me and smiled. "What?" I whispered. She kissed me, and we got swept away for a moment until Susan returned, coughing nervously. We apologized, and she laughed, but the air in the house seemed to have changed somehow.

I don't think Cin noticed, but maybe she did. It was hard to tell how much she picked up on because she was good at acting unphased. She always let things roll off her back, but when we were alone together, her feelings of resentment and pain would catch up with her. Nobody but me saw the side of her that stayed in bed for days at a time, who sometimes looked at kitchen utensils she'd used a million times like they were impossibly complicated pieces of machinery, or that had to walk her through basic tasks when she became overwhelmed. That's why, when I say I knew her better than anyone, I have reason to believe it's true. I saw a side of her that other people didn't see, and sometimes that was a good thing, and sometimes it was hard.

In my own thoughts, I was far from convinced that caring for the birds would be a good long-term job even if it did pay exceptionally well, but it was obvious that Cin was already fascinated by the strange house, Susan, the mysterious necklace.

"I suppose they do take some getting used to," Susan said of the birds, noticing how distracted I had become. "Haven't you ever had a pet canary or anything?"

"She's never had a pet," Cin said, taking a drink of her beer and gently pushing a hand against my arm. "Not even a pup."

"Not even a dog?" Susan asked, mock horrified. "Well, I don't like dogs that much, either. They're awfully loud, aren't they? And kind of, you know...they smell terrible. But not even a hamster? Or a fish?"

"No. I tried to get her to let me adopt a kitten I found once, but...it wasn't to be, I guess."

"First of all, that kitten had rabies."

Cin gasped. "Oh my god! She lies like this. About a kitten! Can you imagine? Sweet, innocent..."

"Diseased, mangy, flea-ridden, bad attitude..."

"Anyway, it's an ongoing conversation, as you can see," Cin explained. "I haven't given up hope, but it'll take a lot more convincing. Maybe we'll just have to wait for the right pet."

Susan was smiling. "Well, it's a lot of work, to be

honest. Taking care of a living thing is always...a lot. It's not for everyone."

Cin's smile changed. She squeezed my arm. "She takes care of me," she said, and Susan took the hint to change the subject. We spent most of the rest of the visit talking about art.

The next time I saw the house, months had passed. Cin had been working there regularly, even covering some shifts for the other caretakers. We had made plans to take the weekend off together, so I came in with her that Friday to help her get through it as quickly as possible. Susan's husband Mark was the one who greeted us that day. He finally came downstairs long after we'd already gotten started. Our clothes were dirty and our hair was disheveled. He hugged us both, though it was the first time I'd met him. The birds were wide-eyed and nervous, a mirror of my own discomfort.

Mark was handsome and gregarious, much the same as Susan. He wore a white suit with a black belt and black shoes. A reddish tint around his brown eyes was the only sign of anything amiss. I dismissed his constant sniffling as allergies, though I later realized he did a lot of cocaine. I should have known, but I was raised by devout Christians and made it to age twenty-three before I'd even tried alcohol, so I was always a bit naive.

Mark brought us drinks and told a few short, inconsequential stories. Eventually, I started to fidget, wondering how long I would have to sit politely in dirty clothes while this guy took up our afternoon with small talk. He finally had to get back to work, so he said goodbye and left the room. Only a couple minutes later, I heard a loud crack. Cin and I ran into the next room. It took a few seconds to register, but there was a window, smashed into pieces.

"Oh," muttered Cin. "Where's Mark? We should let him know."

Outside, there was the sound of a car starting. I walked to the window to see Mark backing out of the driveway. Instinct held me back. Instead of chasing after him, I squinted and tried to get a better look.

"Oh, did we miss him? I'd better text Susan..."

"No," I said. "No, don't. Cin, his hand...it was bloody. I think he did this."

"What? No. Come on. I'm sure he didn't."

We both walked over the mirror as Cin tried to assure me. On the broken glass, there was a splash of blood. I pointed at it, and didn't say anything. Cin's sentence trailed off.

After that, I didn't want Cin to go back there at all. We argued about it a few times until she accused me of trying to hold my financial stability over her head and keep her dependent on me, which made me incredibly angry. I shelved the conversation forever. "Do what you want," I said, and I didn't talk about it any more than that. She seemed compelled to continue working for them regardless of what her instincts were telling her, and I decided then and there that it wasn't worth the struggle. I stubbornly avoided the subject for weeks.

But the birds haunted my dreams.

I wasn't upset that Cin started an affair with Susan. It took me a while to even realize she had. We had both slept with other people before and it always went much the same, with one of us showing up in tears to apologize and swear it would never happen again. Once, several years before, I'd even broken up with her for real when a guy named Steve Carroll my mother had been trying to match me up with since sixth grade proposed to me. Cin had been heartbroken, but that wasn't why I called the engagement off. I just realized that it wouldn't work. I couldn't make it work. When I called her, she'd come back. She always came back.

It was part of our cycle, but this was different. It slowly became obvious that the relationship between Mark and Susan was wearing on them all. Cin seemed more and more fragile.

I have had time to consider how my negligence was its own form of cruelty. In the beginning, there was something about the whole situation that I hoped could be therapeutic for her. I thought she was too needy, too emotional, and that maybe this could help her form meaningful bonds outside of our relationship. I didn't realize how much of that instability was her responding to my calculated indifference. I didn't realize then how much of her pain was caused by me.

I've wondered for a long time why I didn't try to stop her. I'm sure I could have ended it. The opportunity presented itself again and again, but rather than viewing Cin's interest in this strange couple as a threat, I just took it as a vacation during which time I felt blessed to stare at the cracks in the ceiling and think of nothing at all. I thought I finally might get a short break from all the arguments if Cin was being swept away in an illicit affair. Of course it seems callous now, but it's hard to see yourself in the moment sometimes. In my own mind, I was just weary of our repetitions. It didn't even occur to me that what was happening was something new.

One morning, Cin came home shaken and confused. She could barely speak. I pulled her into bed with me, and I wrote off the idea of being able to get any work done. She was breathing heavily, and she was cold, and wet, and she smelled of the sea. I just held her for a long time and waited for her to tell me what had happened. She would start to sit up every now and again, and I would draw her back down, pulling the blanket back over us. I didn't ask her what was wrong. I'd known her long enough to know she would be silent, she might sleep for a while, and then she would talk.

Even after so long, people can still surprise you. She spoke up right as I was writing off any hope of conversation. "There's something wrong with them. Mark and Susan. There's something really wrong with them, you know?"

I sat up, examining her for the first time since she'd gotten home. "Did they hurt you? Are you okay?"

"It's not like that. I mean...deeply, seriously wrong. The stuff with the birds. It's...it's hard to explain, but they...well, Susan...she uses the necklace to...keep them, and...I think she's keeping me the same way. I think she can make people stay. But the birds...want me there. I don't know how to say it other than that. The birds want me..."

"Maybe you should think about quitting," I said abruptly, angrier than I intended to be.

She shook her head, trying to respond but finding herself unable to, and she cried. I apologized, and she absolved me, and we folded into each other like we'd done so many times. That was the last time we did, though. It was the last time things were the same for us. She never tried to open up to me again after that. The next time I held her, she'd become something else entirely.

I tried to convince her not to go back, but by then, she had opened a box she couldn't close.

I only saw Mark and Susan one more time. Well, alive. When I pulled up to drop Cin off, they were standing in the window, in the middle of an argument. When they realized we had arrived, they both turned and stared at us through the foggy glass, not moving. It was immediately off-putting, even if I hadn't already been skeptical about leaving Cin there.

"Are you going to—" I began, but Cin had already gotten out of the car, and the slam of the door cut me short. I sat there, stunned, and eventually let my anger make the choice to back out of the driveway and leave.

There are ways in which we fail the ones we love. Little ways. Small moments where we forget them in our hearts. I failed Cin. I thought of her as a burden. She was crying out for help and I wasn't listening.

There are people that have condemned her for what she became, but not me. I was there. I witnessed first-hand every step as it led to the next—some kind of gravitational life trajectory that we each have, that drags us through moments not of our making and ends, each time, in death.

There are monsters in this story, but Cin was not one of them.

I took the day off, reading quietly and relaxing. When it was time to go pick Cin up, I procrastinated. I thought I just didn't want to see her so soon after our argument that morning, but, looking back, I knew something was wrong that I didn't want to confront.

It had been in the way that she held onto me before she'd left the previous morning, and how she knelt in front of me kissing my fingers that night. We weren't having sex during this time—I think we both intrinsically knew it wouldn't feel right, but we were still sleeping in the same bed. She looked tearfully in my eyes and made me promise that I wouldn't leave her. Again and again, I would say everything she wanted to hear, and I'd add my own flourishes, and in those moments I believed every word. I believed I could be there for her. I believed that was enough.

I would not have guessed how our story together would end. I never could have known that night years before, when she climbed into my bed for the first time, making nervous jokes and touching me too gently, as if she were afraid I would shatter, or draw back, or make her leave. I never would have known then that we would become something so different by the end of it all. While I was trapped in my own existential thought exercises, she was quietly learning new, horrifying things. Things that I will never have to know of, beyond what fragments of them that I saw in her eyes.

From the moment I'd gotten into my car and began the half hour drive up the coastline, I was increasingly anxious. I couldn't handle listening to music and when I put on a podcast the words jumbled together until I became irate and switched the radio off. Instead, I listened to the soft hiss of the cold air coming through the crack between the window and the door, and I worried.

I pulled slowly into the driveway as the sun finally vanished behind the clouds. Both the sky and I were equally hesitant to let go of the daylight. I didn't want the sun to go, and it didn't want to leave me.

I could see the blood immediately, of course. It was all over the windows. I'm sure you've seen the photos. Blood splattering out in the shape of a great bird. The second the car stopped, I jumped out and ran to the door. Whoever was inside would already know I was there from my headlights, so there was no sneaking up, but I wasn't thinking clearly. I pulled the door open, and staggered past the awning.

Inside.

The birds, no longer bound to their posts, hopped and fluttered outside. Mark was laying face down on the floor, dead from a gunshot wound to the head. Susan was in the next room, not visible to me except her hand, which was stretching towards the crystal necklace. Though I would struggle to explain exactly why I did it, I instinctively kicked the necklace away from her, an act that might seem cruel but which I still can't bring myself to regret. Cin's words about Susan and the crystal had seeped into me so that when I saw her grasping for it, my only response was to ensure that she would never touch it again. Without stopping for them, I ran around the house in search of Cin, but I couldn't find her. By the time I returned, Susan's hand had gone limp, and the pendant lay in a pool of blood, chain broken, black eyes glinting.

I called 911, but Cin wasn't found until three days later, hiding in a small enclave on the beach, cold and naked, surrounded by seagulls. She might have been a suspect, but it was immediately obvious under investigation that Susan had shot Mark and had then somehow been pecked to death. They were both covered with claw and bite marks, but not by any of the birds they owned.

Besides that, no one could quite explain Cin's presence, nor the way she'd responded to this tragedy by freeing every bird in the house and roaming the beach like a goddamn wraith for three nights straight. Cin came home to me wrapped in a blanket, completely unresponsive, posing more questions than she could answer. The police said she'd been the same at the station. No matter how often I asked, she would never tell me what had happened. I learned to let it go, but Cin was always a stranger after that.

Months passed. We still shared an apartment, but slept in separate rooms. It sounds heartless, but I couldn't sleep in the same bed knowing that she might start weeping or worse, that I would wake up with her quietly sitting beside me and know that she'd not slept.

"Do you know what it would do to you if I told you what really happened?" Cin asked one night after I had started a half-hearted argument just to get an emotional response from her after weeks of moody silence. "If I told you the things that Susan told me. If you had seen..."

I sat up. "Please, don't go through this alone. Let me go through it with you. Please don't lock me out." Knowing it was too late even as I said it.

She smiled weakly, and touched my face. I tried to get her to open up to me, but she fell asleep while I was talking, and my anger dissolved into despair.

I started seeing a woman named Jessica, which I reasoned was because I couldn't handle Cin's despair. I suppose now I can admit that I was trying to hurt her enough that she would respond to me again. At any rate,

Jessica stopped staying over early on. She complained that Cin sometimes lingered in the doorway while we slept. The last time she stayed the night, we had woken up to Cin sobbing, which turned into a full night of me holding her and attempting to calm her while Jessica angrily waited for dawn to come. The moment the sun appeared on the horizon, she left, and I let Cin fall asleep with her head over my heart like she had so many times before. After that, when Jessica and I spent the night together, it was in the guest bedroom of the home she shared with her husband. I believe it caused some tension between them, but I was completely checked out. I'm sure she didn't deserve that, but in the end, there was no need for anyone to feel badly. I knew this arrangement couldn't last, with Cin and I each giving the other less and less to hold onto. I'd be gone before spring. One way or another, I'd be gone.

When Cin didn't come home for almost four days, I knew I'd have to go after her, but I put it off. It was the final nail in the coffin that I couldn't bear to drive in. The last time I had seen her, she'd acted like her old self, which should have made me feel relieved, but our laughter was too knowing. Roleplaying as our past selves, devoid of the same warmth there once had been. A strange, lifeless caricature, with raw sorrow bursting out from under its surface. I held onto her so tightly, but she might as well have been on another planet.

As my eyes began to close, I noticed something on her chest. A sparkling black eye. The necklace!

I cried out without words, raw anger erupting from my throat. I snapped at her and tried to pull it from around her neck. For the first time in months, she argued with me, telling me that it was none of my business, angry that I had only just noticed when she claimed to have been wearing it for days. I was sure she hadn't been. I was sure Susan had been buried in it. I had seen it around her neck at the funeral. She stormed out and called a car, but I was so infuriated and exhausted by it all that I didn't follow her.

I woke up with a terrible migraine. Cin hadn't come home, and I had to accept that I knew, deep down, where she had gone.

I waited a few more nights before I finally picked the keys up off the counter and walked out to the car. I sat down at the steering wheel and wanted to weep for how terribly I missed the old Cin, who was stronger than me in ways I was only just realizing. The gratingly slow agony of watching her pull away from me over months caught up to me all in a moment. Everything seemed so pointless. Even going to discover the horror that I knew awaited me seemed like nothing more than the next logical step in the excruciatingly long deconstruction of the life we had built together.

The waves were slowly eating away at the last traces of the beach, and only the smallest sliver of sunlight flashed along the horizon, covered in clouds. However far away the sun is, it felt much farther that day, as if once it set it might never return. I stared at the sky for a long time as the light vanished away, leaving only the silhouette of a dark house.

Cin was inside, that much was immediately obvious. She stood in front of the window, nothing more than a shadow but clearly Cin. She sat down on the floor in the empty house, not paying attention to me at all. She was speaking, or chanting, and passionately hitting her palms against the floor for emphasis. I'm sure she knew I was there, but it didn't matter to her.

I heard the cries of birds, and instinctively locked the car doors, watching with absolute awe as dozens, then hundreds, then thousands of shrieking birds covered the property. Birds of all kinds, crowding each other and falling off the sides, lining up through the yard, out to the sea. Crying out, shuffling around, but not causing harm. They overwhelmed my surroundings in less than half an hour while I sat perfectly still and watched them. Cin was yelling something, but it soon became lost in their cacophony. She stood again, and opened the doors wide, letting them inside.

I would hear stories later. Even as I had left every part of my old life behind, people who did not know my connection to the tale would tell me of the shocking story of the girl in the house with the hollow bones, how she had made some kind of an art exhibit from deceased bird bodies she'd found, how they'd found a neighbor on the beach pecked to death by dozens of crows and gulls, and how his house had caught fire in the middle of the night. She never explained any of these things, and eventually vanished from her cell while awaiting trial while flocks of birds fluttered and squawked outside. She was there one moment, and the next, both she and the birds were gone. That was twenty years ago, and she's never been heard from since.

Yet, there have been sightings. Sightings of a woman surrounded by birds, and bodies found along the coastline. Mysteries that have gone unexplained, and I'm afraid I won't be the one to explain them.

I never appear in the stories they tell about her. I think making a note that she had a long-term girlfriend the whole time would throw off the narrative of her as some kind of vengeful bird witch. Urban legends don't have girlfriends, do they? None that I know of, anyway. I'd love to say that two decades later, I have the hindsight to understand what Cin was going through, but I only feel further away from her than ever. Now, she is the subject of articles, podcast episodes, news stories. She even has her own Wikipedia entry, but it's full of errors. Errors that I do not bother to correct.

The story I will never tell is how she wrote me from prison. Long, rambling letters, talking about magic and nature and death. Letters that I read, over and over, even today. The story I will never tell is when I went to see her in jail and how I broke into immediate, ragged sobs. Wanting so desperately to go to her. The story I will never tell is the night when I awoke and she was standing on the other side of our bedroom window, covered in rain and mud, wide-eyed, begging to be let in until the police came and took her back to jail. No one knew how she'd escaped. She told me that she could escape anytime she wanted.

The story I will never tell is how birds follow me to this day, in large, squawking, screaming flocks, covering my house with their bodies, eliciting comments from the neighborhood committee, an inexplicable, quirky thing that they joke about at brunch. I don't talk about the windows I've replaced, the birds I've found squirming in through the walls, the dead bodies I've gotten so used to cleaning up out of my yard that they barely garner a response from me at all. Never attacking me. Always watching me. Always trying to get closer to me.

The story I will never tell is how today I walked outside and found a pendant in the shape of a bird lying on my doorstep. How I hung it around my neck without a second thought, and how the birds screamed as I closed the door behind me.

Because if I told these stories, then it wouldn't surprise anyone to know that I still hear Cin at my window sometimes, scratching at the pane like a bird. Just a bird that I'd let inside, and together we'd locked away the parts of her that scared us. She'd been in a cage I'd helped to build, but now she's free. The door has swung open. I could never close it again.

What I never want to admit was how truly, painfully, shockingly beautiful she had been in that moment, surrounded by death, silhouetted and seeming to hover on the air like a strange forgotten goddess, covered in blood and feathers and somehow freer than she had ever been. How I wanted to go to her, but there was something even more ancient than love that held me back.

Outside the house, watching the birds dance around her, I was jolted back to reality by a crashing sound. A small bird was on the hood of the car. It'd run into the windshield and it seemed hurt, limping slightly and fluttering its wings. I paused for only a moment, then grabbed some napkins and a small box and jumped out to grab the small, feathered thing. It chirped at me, but did not resist. The other birds did not seem to notice us. I started the car, deciding to take it to the vet.

A cloud of black smoke began to billow up over a nearby house, and sirens wailed in the distance. I looked back at the window I'd last seen Cin standing in. She had her hand on the window, finally looking at me. We stared at each other through the smoky gray glass. Slowly, the shadows of birds enveloped her. She disappeared from my sight, and she was gone to me forever. In all the ways that mattered, she was gone.

"Baby," I whispered one final time, and I drove away.

# The Death of a Drop of Water

Rose's fingertips slid down the inside of the window, wet with condensation. Through the rain, in the darkness, she saw the smiles of all the women in white, drenched to the bone, somehow moving closer without moving at all. Surrounded by gray trees, half hidden in the tall grass. She had turned the light off to see them better, but now she'd seen quite enough. She backed up, and flipped the switch again, illuminating the room and lingering in the doorway. It didn't matter if they saw her. They knew where she was, either way. She could hear them moving towards the house in their strange, blinking way, their bodies still as they slid through the gaps between seconds.

Now, she could only see her reflection in the glass, too thin from months and even years of worry. Losing so much and still waiting for the other shoe to drop. Things had been so bad for so long. From the loss of her mother last year, first her character and then her life, to the way her own developing symptoms seemed to mirror hers.

Forgetfulness, anxiety, paranoia. Trying not to notice that her sister, on whom she had always depended, began more and more to pull away from their lives here in their childhood home.

Lightning struck. A woman was pressed against the glass. Thunder roared, covering Rose's scream as she jumped backwards and ran to the kitchen, throwing over the drawers filled with useless tools that would not protect her. She flailed helplessly for only a moment, then worked to calm her breathing. She reminded herself that she needed to keep calm.

Rose started up the stairs. They were everywhere outside. She could see them through the large windows that dotted every side of the house. She ran by the mirror on the wall, but it was a woman in white that passed by on the other side. She paused long enough to throw her palm against the glass, letting out a short, ragged shriek. It shattered. Her hand bled. She looked back. One of them at the bottom of the stairs, and then many of them were, and then just one again. Some of them laughing, some of them crying. They began to climb.

The women had first appeared to her a few days before, in what she supposed was a dream. The day had been hot and humid, and she'd fallen asleep on one of the couches in what was once her grandmother's den. She suddenly found herself in another world, walking through a dying landscape, shuddering from the damp chill soaked through her skin to her bones. It was a strange, petrified forest. Charred, spindly trees jutted into the dark gray sky. The moisture of the air seemed to try and bind to her skin as if it were burrowing in through her pores. It left a film on her skin.

As the initial shock faded, she noticed that there was something wrong with the sounds of the forest. She studied them as she walked, a deep dread rising in her chest. What was it? She listened, baffled by what exactly seemed so wrong. Suddenly, she realized, the sound was backward. From her footsteps to her breathing to the shuffling of the deadened gray grass, the noises were all backward. How was it possible? She tested it, rustled a branch, scraped a shoe across the path, breathed harshly into the air. Backward.

As she neared a great gray lake, she recognized her forest, the forest that surrounded her home, the forest she walked through every day of her life with few exceptions since childhood. Only this place was dead, shadowy, and barren. The trees had no leaves. The sun was absent, leaving a dim haze in its place. That was when she began to suspect that she must be in a nightmare. The thought gave her no moment of comfort, for it was a nightmare that sought to keep her within its clutches indefinitely, until she herself became a part of the dream.

That was when they began climbing up from the water.

The women. All seemingly the same woman, their faces muted and vague in the thick mist. Appearing in slow blinks of time and vanishing again, but always, always moving towards her. It was impossible to tell how many there were. At times, there were none, at times, more than ten. They flashed in and out of existence, but they were all crawling towards her. She stumbled back, trying to grab the branches of the trees to steady herself, but cracked and snapped off, and they were upon her.

They grabbed at her with hands like ice and pulled her toward the lake.

She awoke in a panic, screaming and thrashing until her sobs turned to ragged coughing fits. Normally, her sister, Elizabeth, would have come to help her, but she was traveling and Rose was alone. Since her mother had grown weary of all the illness suffering and drowned herself in the lake, Rose had been alone.

Elizabeth had barely been present over the last few weeks of her mother's life. Rose wondered if her sister would be there when the same thing that happened to their mother happened to Rose, or if she'd be at a party somewhere surrounded by strangers and would get a sudden chill and know that Rose was dead.

She thought about Elizabeth, and their mother, and how those two had been so close to one another that she'd felt jealous of them. Later, when her mother took ill, there had been a distance between them that seemed sudden to Rose. Still, she felt she was on the outside looking in, and couldn't understand their sudden animosity.

Rose often thought of when her mother and her sister would go down by the water, how they would hold hands and sing things in languages that she didn't understand and they wouldn't teach her. She thought of how Elizabeth had looked at her with some pity when they'd return from the lake, like she was just an ill-fated pawn in a chess match that was played behind doors that were forever closed to her. Maybe Elizabeth had known about the women. Maybe she'd helped to call them, and that's why she wouldn't come home.

Though Elizabeth had called her later that day, Rose hadn't told her about the nightmare. She didn't want to spoil her trip. The last time they had spoken about anything serious at all, Elizabeth had said that Rose was too needy, that she held Elizabeth back. The words had splattered over Rose's heart like acid, and she'd burst into tears, hanging up. When Elizabeth called back, she'd choked out an excuse and hung up again. Now, as everything around her was fraying and her world falling apart, she was still trying desperately to prove Elizabeth wrong.

More than anything, Elizabeth had seemed almost relieved when their mother had died. Rose wondered if she would be secretly glad that the wraiths that took their mother had finally come for Rose, and the thought was too much to bear. Elizabeth could be so mean, and she knew exactly what to say and do to cut a person to the core. She was charming, funny, and lovely to be around most of the time, but lately, Rose had seen more of her sister's cruelty than her kindness. She wondered what Elizabeth knew about the women, but she was afraid to ask.

As the days dragged by, the women began appearing to her during the day as well as the night, always drawing closer and closer. She had no doubt that they were coming from her mother's lake, which had become her lake when her mother had died. She would watch them from the windows while they were still far out in the choppy waters, but when they had gotten closer than that, Rose had shut the curtains. It must have been the rain that finally brought them to the porch. Like pale nightcrawlers, rising from the mud, they crept closer.

Tonight, they'd come inside, uninvited and unwanted, as if the heavy oak doors did not exist. She pushed all the furniture in the bedroom in front of the door, but she could still hear them outside, speaking backwards. It was impossible to understand what they were saying, but they talked all through the night in their strange, grinding version of language. Rose tried to stay awake, but she had barely slept in all this time. Exhaustion lay on her chest like a heavy brick, and she slowly drifted into sleep, finally falling into a dream of stillness and silence.

When she awoke the next morning, it was to a ringing phone. It took her some time to locate the landline, which she had never used and didn't realize was still in service. She could almost hear Elizabeth's chiding tone. "What a waste of money!"

Rose agreed that it was a waste of money, but nobody told her about it, so she wasn't sure what she could have done. That was how things always were with Elizabeth. She would wait for anything to go wrong and blame it on Rose, but not directly. In a sort of condescending undertone. Rose lifted the receiver, and began to say "hello."

A voice on the other side shrieked, in the same backwards way she had in her dream. Rose slammed the receiver back down, but the sound continued until it filled the house. Rose hid under the bed with her hands over her face and sobbed.

After some time, the noise subsided, and she finally crawled out. She walked to the window, the blinds still drawn closed like they had been the night before. Hesitantly, she reached to the drawstring, and began to pull. The cloth crinkled and rose up, soundless and smooth. She drew it up halfway, then paused, taking a deep breath before her wrist jerked downward. The curtain lifted and revealed the world to her.

Rose gasped. The women were everywhere. She was

back in the dead world from her dream. They could see her. She kicked backwards and fell, head crashing against the floor, and, once again, she was asleep.

When she came to once more, her head was throbbing. She scrambled to stand up. Looking out of her window, everything appeared to be normal. A sunny afternoon, with storm clouds forming at the edge of the horizon. She placed a hand over her mouth to stifle a sob. Not another night of rain. She wanted to pray for help, but there was no one to pray to when the weather started to come down as it did. Not even God could stop the storm.

Rose grabbed her shawl and walked out into the yard, tears streaming down her face. She strode out into the field and yelled at the sky, her voice eaten up by the wind. She put every bit of her misery into her voice and wailed at the clouds, but she still gasped when she felt drops of rain on the back of her hands. She looked at them, and then to the lake. A soft backwards moaning appeared under the wind. Rose's anger shifted, faded, and turned to fear. She turned, and ran back up the stairs, bolting the door shut.

She sat at the dining room table, smoking a pack of cigarettes out of her mother's stash. The smokes were stale, but they were complemented by the richly aged whiskey that she'd found next to them. She ashed into a teacup, knowing it would make her mother and her sister absolutely furious to see her now. Not just for the lack of manners. She glanced around. This was a highly flam-mable house, after all. The long cloth curtains, oversized paintings, expensive rugs, and old wiring made for a dangerous mix. She supposed she didn't have to care about that, now.

Rose had considered calling her sister and begging her to come home, but the condescending tone with which Elizabeth would surely respond was more than she could take. More than anything, she wished her sister could be gentle with herself, and that it might help her be more gentle to others. Elizabeth couldn't come home right now, not in the way that mattered. Rose felt it was futile to drag her into this mess.

That was the problem, after all, Rose thought as the shadows grew and the sunlight faded. The overwhelming sense of futility hanging over her head. If she escaped, she would still be ill, wouldn't she? She'd still just end up like her mother; dead, in a coffin. Elizabeth would leave soon, maybe to get married or maybe just to live in the city like she always said she wanted. Who, then, would be left for Rose to talk to? Who would stay by her side, besides nurses?

She knew she was being defeatist, but she'd seen the face of the woman crawling to her, and the face may as well have been her mother's, and it may as well have been her own.

Rose heard a noise outside, and took one final drink to fortify herself. Then, she strode to the front door, pushing it open. The women were approaching from far away. This time, with wind and rain and darkness in her eyes, she watched them come.

Once they had gotten nearly to the door, Rose leaped forward and ran outside. She bolted past them, their boney, grabbing hands, through the slick, sharp grass of the field, into the forest. Blades of grass sliced at her legs, and thin ribbons of blood blossomed down her calves.

The women screamed in layers, shrieking as she darted through the woods.

The lake was in sight. Her lake. Not the still lake of a dead world but a swaying, living body of water teeming with life even under the gray and black sky. The women were nearly on top of her once more. Rose thought of everything—the pain, feeling inconsequential, needing people who did not need her, and with a final scream, she ran down the dock and leapt with her full body into the dark waters. In the last moment as she fell towards the water, she saw her mother, laughing, her arms stretched out wide to welcome her. She screamed, her body suddenly struggling against its own leap, as she crashed into the lake.

It seemed so sudden that she opened her eyes once more. It was morning. How was that possible? She remembered dying, or at least something like dying. She breathed a sigh of relief to know she had survived the night. Yet, when she looked down, she saw that she was dressed all in white, like the women from the water's edge. Thick black liquid lapped against the walls of her bedroom. She was soaked all the way through, covered in it. The phone rang again. Rose opened her mouth to cry out, but hands rose from the water, gripping her arms and legs. They pulled her down, under the oily surface, deeper and deeper. Darkness fell over her, and for long, terrible moments, everything was excruciatingly silent.

In another world, rising from a dead lake under a great black sky, she dragged herself to the shore. She collapsed on the sharp rocks, and screamed, and sobbed, and ripped at her own flesh. Through the reflection of the lake, she could see herself on the other side, picking up the phone and calling Elizabeth to come home. She looked away, burying her face in her hands, unwilling to watch any longer. The petrified trees did not move with the breeze. Except for her, there was no sound. In this dead world, she was alone, and every noise she made, it came out backward.

# A SMALL LIGHT

WHEN I GOT TO CHOOSE OUR VACATION, WE VISITED several landmarks and a half dozen museums in Paris and Berlin. This was mutually allowed on the condition that if we splurged, our next trip would be more reserved. A year later, it was time to pay the piper. While I was on the phone with my wife Ashley's mother one night, she suggested that we stay at their cabin in Northern California for a week or two. Ashley seemed reluctant at first, but her mom insisted, and I agreed, more to tease Ashley than out of sincere interest. When the call ended, I realized what I had done – we were going to be going camping for a whole week of our lives, and it was all my fault.

I had never even actually been camping, but I didn't mention that to Ashley. Camping was a natural part of her life. I don't think it would have crossed her mind that a person could just live their whole lives and never once sleep outdoors by choice. It might have been our different backgrounds, she'd been part of a wholesome suburban family unit while I'd lived in the middle of a city with an overworked single mother and three other siblings. I had never spent much time in the woods at all, and I was fine with that. I'd rather read a book at home, or go see a movie, or just stay in bed. Truly, anything other than camping would be fine.

I didn't mention my predisposition against all things nature, not because I didn't want to upset Ashley, but because I wanted to give her my participation with no strings attached, as she had always done for me. Even if I was secretly bemoaning the trip, I didn't want to assume I would hate it. Maybe I wouldn't. Maybe we would just spend the whole time talking and having sex and, sure, sometimes hiking the daunting route she had mapped out for us. Anything was possible, I reasoned. Here, in my 30s, I might just finally become the kind of lesbian that loves camping all of a sudden. Maybe I would buy my first flannel shirt. The sky was, truly, the limit.

This was the sincere hope I had murmured when my friends looked at me, appalled, and cried out, "YOU? CAMPING?" as if the very idea entailed a forbidden merging between diametrically opposed concepts that could only end in catastrophe. "As long as my beloved wife is with me, it'll be lovely," I said with a level of sincerity that couldn't help but sound like bullshit. My friends moaned. We eventually left the bar. Life moved along. Ashley made plans. I dreaded the moment, but the day of our departure finally came.

I ate an edible before we got in the car, so I have to admit that the drive there was amazing. Ashley was incredibly attractive to me all day, even more so than usual. I gazed at her admiringly as she took charge, helped me pack, got us out the door on time. She calmly and confidently drove us out of the city and into the woods, listening to a lot of shoegaze bands that I couldn't tell apart but she could, and occasionally mentioning fun facts about landmarks as we cruised along. My heart ached. I had married not just a gorgeous, talented woman, but also an amatuer tour guide. I was so lucky. I couldn't stop staring at her hands gripping the steering wheel as shadows from the trees overhead shifted and danced across her skin. I knew the first night would be in the cabin, so I already had my mind fully invested in our night together, completely alone and far away from thin walls and the prying ears of our overcrowded apartment complex.

It was like a dream, and it didn't end when she stopped the car and showed me the home-away-from-home that had defined so much of her childhood. Up on a steep, rocky hill overlooking a lake, surrounded by tall trees, there was a small cabin. This was where my Ashley spent her summers as a girl. It was so wholesome. I spent my preteen years trying to look cool in front of older girls and bumming cigarettes at house shows while she was out here roasting marshmallows around a campfire. What a nerd. I blushed with love for her.

After a quick tour of the property, she pulled me inside and pushed me against the wall, and we made love on-and-off for most of the rest of the day. She was so beautiful that night, smoking a cigarette out on the balcony and telling me things I'd never known about her. The stress of her job was completely gone from her eyes, and she laughed loudly with me, and we drank wine and whispered sweet things to each other until early in the morning.

It was late in our evening when I had got around to the question I'd been waiting to ask. Of the two of us, I was always the one that thought every place we visited was haunted. Ashley always disagreed, so I was half teasing her skepticism when I attempted a casual tone and asked, "Um... did you ever see any ghosts here?"

Ashley laughed. "I knew you were going to ask! You always do this! You're so morbid!"

"I'm morbid, or the world is morbid?"

"You are. You want to know because... why? What will you get out of it? I'll tell you what I'll get out of it—you, waking me up in the middle of the night because you're having nightmares."

"No," I lied. "I'm brave now."

"Since when? Last week?"

"Since all year. You just didn't notice. I never have bad dreams anymore."

"Why not?"

"Some would say I conquered them by sheer force of will, but I personally would give all the credit to my beautiful wife, who selflessly supported me from day one."

Ashley rolled her eyes. "Flattery will get you nowhere you haven't already gotten before." She glanced down over my body, lingering for a while before taking my hand and looking back into my eyes. "Well, I can tell you... there's a story of a woman in the woods. Local kids told me. They had a lot of stories of her... some of us saw her. If she was even real, she... she was probably just a woman who lived alone out here somewhere, but we had stories. My friend told me that she caught up to him by the river and told him when he was going to die. He was never the same after that. He... he died not too long after."

"Baby. That sounds... incredibly made up."

Ashley looked serious. "Well, you know about my... I... also had a friend go missing when we were kids. Belle. My first girlfriend. You know, we all genuinely thought it was the witch that took her. Like... how kids make things up to make themselves feel better. I'm sure she must have just run away... or... been kidnapped, or..."

She was silent for a moment, so I broke in, "Well, if the witch comes after us, I'll protect you. I can almost definitely take an elderly woman in a fight."

"I... " Ashley began, and looked like she was about to say something else, but she rolled her eyes instead, squeezing my shoulders. "I'd like to think so, but these arms are like putty."

"Who needs to use arms to win in a fight? My strength is my mind. I'm incredibly gifted in the art of negotiation, you know."

She grinned. "You really are," she agreed, kissing my throat. "You really are."

The second day... is the day when we should have stayed in bed, called the whole thing off, and did absolutely everything in our power to avoid continuing this horrible, terrible, no-good very bad trip. If we hadn't had such a sweet, relaxing night, maybe we'd have been more inclined to take a second day of luxurious peace and quiet together. Instead, she was up at the crack of dawn, gathering our backpacks and making tofu scramble for breakfast.

I tried to start the coffee but she stopped me, handing me a cup. "Here."

"Thank you," I mumbled, kissing her cheek.

"No problem, I didn't want you fumbling around in here pre-caffeine while I'm trying to cook. Sit down! We'll eat on the porch."

I obliged, reading a teen magazine from the '90s while waiting to be served. We ate together, basking in the sunlight, listening to the lake and the rustle of the leaves. Eventually, Ashley stood up, a little abruptly.

"We should get going."

The hike itself was brilliant. Again, this is likely because I was high on edibles, but even with an abundance of THC in my system I could recognize that our surroundings were truly something to see. It was sunny, and there was a nice breeze. Branches jostled and swayed overhead. Ashley told various anecdotes about her family and their time hiking together, and I listened to her soothing voice without interrupting much. We stopped a few times to lay in the grass to kiss, but in the end I got tired much earlier than Ashley did. She was walking too quickly for me and seemed nervous and even a little agitated, but she was always so good at hiding her feelings that I couldn't tell for sure. We'd never been on such a long hike together before, so I didn't know if this was just how she got, but her eyes darted through the trees again and again.

By early evening, Ashley was ready to set up camp. It was a place she knew well—there was a beautiful, grassy clearing near a river and a tree carving of the name of her preteen friend-turned-secret-girlfriend turned-lost-love, Belle. She left the tent and supplies with me while she went to go find some wood for a fire.

She didn't come back. I waited and I waited. I tried to

stay calm. I stared at the carving in the tree and wondered what Ashley's other relationships had been like before she had formed into the person that married me. I half-smiled thinking of how bad her game must have been when she was a teen suburbanite trying to impress cool wilderness girls. Even those thoughts couldn't fully distract me from the fact that she had been gone for far too long.

The dread started to creep in. She said fifteen minutes, but over an hour eked by with nothing. The sun was going down. I got worried. I paced. The high from the edibles was gone, and I started to crash. I took steps out into the field, trying to get a better vantage point to look for her. I scanned the tops of the trees, and the hills in the distance. Nothing. I squinted. Nothing.

Nothing.

No. Not nothing. Something. A figure moving along a path in the hills, far from me but close enough to be barely seen. I waved my arms, calling out, "Ashley!"

I realized then that the person in the hills was not Ashley. They looked right at me, their eyes glowing like a cat's. I gasped and put both hands over my mouth. The figure moved quickly, too quickly, out of my line of sight. I staggered backwards, looking frantically around me. I needed to find Ashley. Immediately.

"Sandra!" Ashley's voice. I turned, my heart thundering. She was heading towards me from the woods, carrying kindling in her arms.

"Where were you?" I cried. "What happened? I thought you were gone!"

"I thought the same about you! Where did you go?"

"I didn't go anywhere! I was waiting for you!"

"No! I came back already. You moved."

"I didn't! I've been here!"

She shook her head, biting her lip. "How weird. I know it was the spot. The tree with my carving. I've been here a million times. I know it like the back of my hand." She frowned, looking into the distance, searching the treeline with her eyes. "I was afraid for you. I thought something had happened. Come here."

I trotted over to her. We embraced in the sunset, but I couldn't forget the glowing eyes I had seen on the horizon, and I was afraid. I tried to tell her, but it sounded absurd when I actually said it out loud. She simply shrugged and said that we were bound to cross paths with someone on the trail. I was sure it was my imagination. They must have just been wearing glasses. I told myself all of the repetitive phrases we say to rationalize the things that we don't want to be true, but the worry never left my mind again that night.

We had the supplies to make a fire, but it wasn't much longer until dark clouds rolled in overhead and we were hit hard by an unforeseen storm. Ashley assured me that the news had expected fair weather for the week. In our small tent, it felt like a hurricane. The tent was waterproof, but the storm was harsh. We cuddled together. Ashley quickly fell asleep, but moaned and thrashed uncomfortably. I held her, and worried.

I drifted into my own fitful slumber when I heard a soft noise under all the rainfall. At first, I thought it was nothing more than Ashley's troubled sleep noises, but it was coming from far away. A soft, gentle singing, in the distance but getting closer. It was so hushed that the words were unintelligible, but it seemed to be coming from all sides at once. I looked out through the cracks in our makeshift tent. At first, I saw nothing but the rain and the trees, but after a moment, a small light.

My eyes drifted in and out of focus as I began to realize how tired I was. My body was slowly shutting down against my will. I fortified myself and tried to get a clear look. There should be no light. My heart began to thunder.

It was getting closer. The song was impossible to make sense of, but it seemed to get even louder as I tried in vain to hear it over the heavy drops falling all around. Rain gathered on my eyes and my face, and I tried to rub it away with dirty hands. The light was larger and larger. I began to panic, but weariness called me to lay back down. Though I fought it, I was falling asleep. It was the singing. The singing was putting me to sleep.

I pushed aside the flap. The light had gotten much larger now, much closer. It was human-shaped, but not yet human, steadily walking towards us. My stomach lurched with dread as I realized that I wasn't going to be conscious for long. Despite how hard my heart was beating, my eyes could barely stay open. "Please no," I whispered, and tried to wake Ashley. She must have been stricken with the same spell as me, because her eyes fluttered and rolled, but would not open. I tried to put my hands over my ears to force the song out, but it was too strong.

The last thing I saw was a woman, radiating light, her features distorted, reaching her hand into our tent. As I fell face forward in the dirt, fading to unconsciousness, her bright glowing hand gripped Ashley's ankle and dragged her away from the tent. I tried to shriek, tried to grab Ashley's wrist, but my hand crashed into the cold wet dirt and the darkness consumed me.

When I woke up, I was screaming, leaping out of the sleeping bag, kicking over the tent, leaving everything behind. It was morning, but still dark and damp. Clouds covered the sun. I called out for Ashley. I ran in circles, cried, and panicked. I walked to the center of a great field, and sobbed.

When she finally walked up to me, at first I couldn't process what I was seeing. Ashley, covered in leaves and mud, striding across the field. I leapt to my feet and ran for her, and we held each other and wept.

Ashley pointed across the field, into the trees. "I woke up there. In the woods. I woke up... what happened?"

I quickly told her what I had seen, and how I had fallen asleep. She was weak and wobbly, so we sat on the wet ground. We kissed and clung to each other. She was scraped and bruised, as if she'd actually been dragged across the field. I ached with guilt. I wished I could have fought the person that took her, but how could I have? She eventually suggested that we grab our things and head back to the house, and I agreed on the condition that we could also drive the Hell out of there the second we made it to the front steps.

Ashley looked haggard. She threw up more than once. Eventually, we happened upon an old rowboat on the bank. She suggested that we ride as far as we could back towards the cabin. It didn't look like she had the strength to walk. I was shaking with fear, terrified that she would take a turn and I'd be unable to help. I spent the morning on the verge of sobbing.

I tried to be brave. I pushed us outward, along with the

current. We were going fast, which scared me because I had no idea how to stop us once we made it as far as we could go. Ashley didn't seem worried. She was out of it. She laid her head on my lap.

"I saw her, you know," Ashley murmured. I immediately knew that she was talking about the woman made of light. My hands stroked her hair gently. I didn't speak. She continued. "I saw her... I saw her. I saw Belle. I think I saw her again last night... I think I saw her, but... all made out of light..."

My stomach was doing flips, but I kept rubbing her temples. "Baby," I said gently, "just rest."

She shook her head, tears forming in the corners of her eyes. "We looked and looked when she went missing, but we never found her. I've been out here a dozen times since then, and I never saw her again. I thought..." She held my hand tightly. "I could ignore it when I heard the soft singing that sounded like her. I thought I... I thought I was imagining it all. I thought I had made it up. But I didn't, did I? You saw her."

I frowned, and looked around, scanning the trees for any movement. Even then, it felt like there were eyes on us, but I saw nothing. I looked back down at her, and forced a slight, strained smile. "No. I didn't. We're almost home. We'll be home soon."

"I don't think Belle died," Ashley said through tears. "I think... I think she became... something else."

Ashley fell asleep on my lap as we drifted down the river. An hour passed. The skies were overcast. The branches overhead hung heavy with the moisture from the night before. I jumped at every sound, but eventually I grew tired. Yawning, once, then again, and again. My heart began to pound as I realized that I should not be so tired as I was.

I saw a movement out of the corner of my eye.

So convinced was I that I would see nothing when I turned that it took seconds for me to fully register what I actually was seeing. The woman, blond-haired, in a white dress, with glowing eyes, an aura of light around her, creeping towards us from behind the trees. Her song began again, detached and inhuman, but unmistakably hers. She was hunched slightly, but took long, sweeping steps, her legs stretching further than legs could stretch. She reached the water's edge in seconds. I expected her to stop, and gasped when she did not hesitate to walk right into the water. I tried to grab for the oar, but my body started giving way to sleep. Again, I shook Ashley, and again, she would not wake. I squawked and fumbled desperately, but the energy drained from my body.

Her eyes stayed fixed on me as she waded towards us, unbelievably fast. Her head stayed above water and she did not seem to be swimming, but she cut through the water like a knife. I continued to sob as I shook Ashley and weakly called her name.

The woman's head disappeared underneath the surface. I looked all around, crying out. The singing rose up all around me, growing louder and louder. I pushed my palms over my ears, and sobbed.

Suddenly, there was a loud crash. She clutched the side of the boat. Long, broken fingernails and blue-tinted skin. Her face appeared over me, eyes glowing, her expression hateful and otherworldly. She began to open her mouth, and there was nothing inside. No teeth, no tongue. A void.

I didn't have the strength to scream as I lost consciousness once more.

I opened my eyes. Ashley was gone. I shrieked, and wept. I tried to stand, but I was too unsteady and fell back into the bottom of the boat, which was filling slowly with water. I looked around frantically, kicked my hoodie and my shoes off, and jumped into the water. It was freezing, as if it were the middle of winter, and I hadn't braced myself for it. I didn't have time to think then that the water should not have been so cold in the first week of September.

I dragged myself up the bank, searching for any sign of Ashley. I screamed her name until I was hoarse. Where had she gone? The woman couldn't have carried her all the way back to the shore, could she? If Ashley had fallen under, she was already dead. I thought of her cold and alone at the bottom of the river, her eyes wide open, never to close again. I clawed at my arms and hated myself for falling asleep.

Over my sobs, I heard singing.

I jumped to my feet, eyes searching the woods. I saw a small light, at the mouth of what looked like a cave. The woman, dragging something behind her. I recognized Ashley's shoe. She was pulling Ashley into the cave by the leg. I couldn't tell if she was dead or alive. Another pang of pain and terror shot through me, and I trembled so hard my vision blurred.

It seemed impossible that the woman could drag her so easily. Exerting so little effort. I screamed, guttural and raw. "No!" Rage surged in my heart, and I bolted up the side of the hill after them, growling like an animal, with no caution whatsoever. I was so infuriated at the idea of anyone moving Ashley around like an object that anger consumed me and made me forget my fear.

I made it to the mouth of the cave, and saw the woman dragging Ashley further. I ran inside, and was hit by an overpowering inertia, as if the air were quicksand, dragging me down. I struggled to put one foot in front of the other. This was exactly the way I'd felt in the tent, and in the boat. Still, I kept going, terrified that I would lose my wife to this ungodly nightmare creature. I fell and my legs bled, but I forced myself back up and kept staggering forward.

When I had nearly reached them, the woman turned and opened her mouth once again, screaming so powerfully that it seemed to come from all sides at once. It knocked me to my knees, but I grabbed Ashley by the other ankle. I crawled over her, putting my entire body over hers. "No!" I growled again, blood from my ears dripping onto the dirt.

The woman made no motion. Slowly, I opened my eyes to look, and screamed again. Her face was right next to mine. Her eyes were glossy and dead, but seemingly lit from within by a cold blue flame. Her lips moved, but they did not match the warbled, unintelligible words that came. Her mouth began to open wide. So, so wide. I shut my eyes and waited for the end.

What happened after that, I could not say. A couple that had braved the rainy day for a short hike found us. I had shrieked so loudly that they had heard it from half a mile away. I'd still been screaming for help and holding onto Ashley for dear life when they'd found us. They'd called rangers, and the rangers had called the police, and the police called an ambulance, and we were taken back to the city. After a couple weeks, Ashley's brother Todd brought us Ashley's car and what was left of our things.

We were both so dehydrated that we were on the brink of death. They said it would have taken days with no water to cause such a state. In another couple hours, we'd have died. Ashley and I simply listened and nodded, numb, while the doctors gave us useless advice about bringing sports drinks next time and staying hydrated. As if there would ever be a next time. The police found our clothes shredded and arranged in strange patterns on the shore of the river. They attempted to return them to us, but I threw them away.

The months that followed were fraught. Neither of us could sleep. Our therapists didn't believe our stories, so they couldn't help us cope. We took too many sick days, and Ashley had to switch jobs to take a lower pay grade when she lost her patience and walked out of a meeting. We were still committed to each other, but struggling. Rather than opening up, neither of us could talk about it at all. Our communication suffered. Ashley rarely smiled, and I jumped at every noise.

She told me only a little more about Belle's disappearance. How she had watched her disappear into a cave and had never seen her again. No. How she'd seen her once more, but she'd been so certain it was a dream. Scraping on the outside of her window, singing softly. Pleading with her to come outside, to come back to the cave, to stay with her there forever.

Today, it is one year later. I can't stop looking out the window, terrified that I will see glowing blue eyes staring back at me.

Ashley came home from work about an hour ago. She

took a shower and changed into her robe. She made dinner for us, and we ate, mostly in silence. She went into the living room, and sat down in her favorite chair, sighing so deeply that my heart ached with sympathy and I couldn't help but go to her.

I stand in the doorway and stare at her, thinking of how much I love her, how vulnerable and afraid I feel, how unable to protect her I was, and how hard it has been on us both to struggle through this. How sometimes I'm afraid that we're losing touch with each other. How scared I am that we will never bounce back from this.

Before I can decide on what I want to say to her, she speaks up. "I'm so sorry, Sandra," she says, not looking at me but knowing I am there. "I'm so sorry I took you back there with me. I'm so sorry for everything."

"You don't have to be sorry." I shrug and look at the floor. I feel that she might not have known that. I might not have shown her. I immediately wish I'd told her before, you don't have to be sorry. "I should have..." I start, but I let the sentence fall away from me.

In the background, under the noise of the city, I hear soft, gentle singing.

I'm hit by a wave of nausea and weariness, and I know we don't have long. I walk over to Ashley. She watches me warily and seems afraid of me, or afraid I might leave, or maybe even afraid of herself. I realize now that there is so much I don't know. So much I've been afraid to ask. Does Belle still whisper to her in the night? Has she come to see me as a burden? Does she resent me for keeping them apart? Is this the day that she finally opens the window and lets her in? I look into my wife's watery eyes, and it's hard for me to say for sure what she's feeling. I smile weakly at her until she smiles back, but I can tell we both want to cry. I take a tentative step forward, then drop to my knees. I kiss her hands, and I rest my head on her legs.

Ashley doesn't move for a long time. Then I feel her hand, gently touch the back of my head, stroking my hair. Her fingers tighten around the base of my ponytail. The singing gets closer. A small light gets bigger.

# Red Lips in a Blue Light

One thing she appreciated was that the studio was dimly lit. She'd lost her taste for bright lights as a young girl. They gave her a headache. On her third day of work, she had nervously asked the men behind the mirror to dim them and they had complied. Now, when she entered the studio, the lights were off, and she could set them herself. They had changed the color from glaring white to a soothing blue.

They were nearly done for the day. She had two stacks of paper, the one on the right was the things she had already read and the one on the left was the pages she had left. The left had dwindled until she was down to just one. She lifted the last piece up with both hands. She scanned it and waited for them to speak.

"So, what do you do for fun?" one of the men asked.

She set the paper down on top of the others. "It's actually really funny," She smiled. "I'm really a very private person. Despite the popularity I have experienced this last year with you all, in my regular life, I'm... well, I'm painfully shy. My favorite activity is just to curl up and read a book. Or, more often than not, a catalog."

The men chuckled, and she nodded and bowed to them, even though she couldn't see them from her side of the glass. She could just see herself, basking in a blue glow.

There was some minor discussion after this, but eventually, they said it would be fine for her to go home. She was relieved. It might have been just another script, but she did get so anxious when she had to be out of her house for more than a few hours.

She was used to seeing herself on screens. Everywhere She looked, there she was, the recordings of the previous Sunday morning flashing across the landscape of the city. She had to walk around in scarves and long coats and wide-brimmed hats to avoid being noticed when she left her 15th-floor apartment. One blessing of the job is that she didn't have to be outside for long.

Only Sundays and Wednesdays did she really have to go out in order to go back inside to sit in front of the cameras and microphones in Studio 31. There, she would record pages of disconnected dialogue that sometimes sounded like nothing more than incoherent rambling as she tripped over her own tongue trying to say it all. She would read straight from the teleprompter, stare into the camera, pout or smile depending on what she felt was appropriate, and after several hours, she would leave. Some days, it was easy. Some days, it was hard.

She had gotten the job only a year before, but it had long since become a monotonous grind. She imagined anything would eventually be that way. The job also happened to be all she had. She had been struggling

desperately when she'd been hired and it was a godsend.
Who wouldn't want to be one of the most famous women
in the city? They took care of everything. All of her
expenses. They sent her food in little boxes so she didn't
have to shop. They paid for her apartment with only one
window, dimly lit and secluded at the end of the hall.

They offered her a car, but she preferred the train. The
drivers of the cars would always talk too much, too freely,
in that way that she had never quite mastered. She had
been raised all alone, with doctors and nurses and
teachers and therapists, but no friends, and it had stuck
with her. She'd never really had a friend to this day,
although she had tried. Most people were raised alongside
other people, and it was obvious that this difference alien-
ated her. She had been raised by people that always left by
5 p.m. In the night, if she wanted company, she had to
scream and make a racket, but she learned quickly that
they didn't like it when she did that. They punished her by
tying her to her bed only one time, and she never did it
again.

She waited patiently for the train she needed. She had
agreed she would meet the man tonight, but she was
already regretting it. The man had shown up quite
valiantly one day a few months ago, helping her across the
street when she was having an anxiety attack, soothing
her. He worked in the same building as her, she realized
and was disturbed to be recognized in public by anyone,
let alone a man. He had invited her to dinner, and she had
gone. It felt like the correct thing to do. He was charming,
and she knew that other women found him attractive and
funny. It just didn't quite click for her. Then again,
nothing ever really seemed to.

She would continue seeing him if he wanted to. She didn't have anything better to do. She would stay inside under a blanket and watch herself on TV, or watch brooding melodramas, and exercise sometimes. Usually, she remembered to eat. She had thought about getting a cat but was afraid that something would happen to it. Besides, she wasn't sure quite what to do with a cat. The same she did with the man, she would sit and observe it with mild terror, she assumed.

A young girl and her mother were next to her on the train. She tried not to stare, but she couldn't help it. They touched each other's hands and smiled so warmly. She wanted to join them, but she wouldn't know how to be a mother, or a daughter, really. They hadn't offered her any classes on that.

She paused for a moment, considering. Mother. This was a word she knew. Why had she never wondered about its meanings? Nobody she knew really talked about their mothers in this grey city under the black and red sky. All she really remembered before it was a sterile, cold, clinical youth spent within the blank walls of a building no one ever really explained to her.

Of course, she had a mother, but it wasn't like this. It wasn't warm. It was the woman in the white room, surrounded by gauzy curtains, tubes running out of her into machines flanking her on either side, perpetually pregnant. Not a mother, really, so much as a distant goddess. She was happy to see her for the few moments that were allowed, but these were only brief, fleeting memories in between a childhood that was wrapped in cellophane and lit by overhead fluorescent bulbs.

Still, she missed her. Once she had heard someone say,

"you can't miss something you never had," but she was certain that wasn't true. Her heart had grown only increasingly, desperately hungry for it. For anyone to smile at her the way the mother smiled at the daughter on the train.

She had never spoken to her mother, but once she had held her for an extra few seconds and kissed her forehead before she was carried out of the room by staff. It was the only time someone had held onto her. She still remembered. She would always remember.

On television, she saw herself say the words, "my mother passed away when I was only a child. We buried her on the hill in the cemetery overlooking the sea."

She paused. She had never said that. She was sure of it. More and more, quips and phrases that she distinctly knew she would have disagreed with were popping up in the transmissions. "Are they doctoring the footage?" she wondered, "but why would they?" There had only been a handful of phrases in all this time that she'd declined. One card said, "I remember how my father would kiss my mother's forehead before sitting down with us for dinner every night." One had said, "My mother is the most beautiful woman I've ever seen."

The whole point of her was that she didn't know her parents well enough to say anything about them at all. Her father may never have existed. She wasn't totally sure how childbirth worked now, but it didn't seem anything like what she'd read in books. In the city, sometimes people had fathers, but she had no idea who or what had been hers. She wanted to, though. It was another thing she kept in her mind to ask her mother if she ever saw her again.

The line itself had been true. Her mother was truly beautiful, that was undeniable. Like an angry God in the sky, she was serving a terrible, necessary purpose. She represented one view of truth that was elemental and unsettling. It had been true in a way that had made her too uncomfortable to say out loud. Her mother really was the most beautiful woman she'd ever seen. She just couldn't say the words.

She had agreed to meet the man in front of the cafe where they always met. It was raining, so she had backed up to wait under the awning. Immediately, the restaurant workers had demanded to know why she was dallying, so she explained, and they reluctantly agreed to allow her to wait. He appeared in the crowd of people walking down the street, and broke into a jog, rushing up to her. He kissed her cheek and brushed some of the rain off of them both.

"Did you get your work done?"

She nodded. "Yes, I…" she thought about it. "I did."

"Great! So you can come with me tonight."

She nodded even more slowly, almost smiling, deciding against it, then going for it, perhaps too great a smile, perhaps too enthusiastically. "Yes!"

"Is there something the matter?"

She shook her head, thought about it, then nodded. "I just think… maybe they're getting angry with me, or… maybe I'm not saying the lines correctly, anymore."

"You're the It Girl, aren't you?" he smirked, somewhat cruel, then becoming self-aware of the cruelty, his smirk faded and he glanced away and back again. He raised his eyebrows as if he'd asked an honest question that warranted a serious response.

"What does that even mean?" She wondered. "We're all constantly using phrases when we have no clue what they mean. Where did that term come from? Even the reporter that called me that had no idea. I asked. I wrote to her. She didn't know."

He sighed, seeming bored. "If you wear yourself out asking pointless questions, you'll be too tired to do anything else," he warned without realizing what a relief it would be to her not to have to go with him tonight.

She smiled with superficial tolerance, suddenly angry with him. "I'm actually not feeling well. Do you mind if I don't go?"

He rolled his eyes. "I knew you were going to cancel. You always cancel."

"I never agreed to begin with. I said..."

"Wait and see," he finished in a sing-song tone, mocking her. "It's what you always say. Well, go on, I don't want to catch whatever you've got, anyway." They still ate dinner with each other. When it was over, he kissed her cheek, and they walked away from one another. He tried to light his cigarette in the rain and ended up losing it to the wind while she walked evenly and gracefully with no jacket and no umbrella through the black raindrops that fell heavily from the sky.

She began wandering, uncertain of where exactly she intended to go. Surprising even herself, she darted into the subway tunnel and scanned the pending trains. There was one bus she hadn't caught in years, not since it had brought her here, to the city. One specific bus, that only went to a single place, with only a few stops along the way. The bus that could take her to her mother, and where she'd come from.

It didn't make sense. She wouldn't be allowed to see her mother. She hadn't been allowed before when they lived under the same roof and it would be worse now. She was fairly convinced she could even get in trouble for it.

Still, she couldn't stop thinking of her mother. She just couldn't. There wasn't anything else in her life. There wasn't anyone. She had bounced from room to room and building to building for years. It was all she really knew. To her, other people had always seemed intrusive and loud. It gave her nausea and headaches to be around too many of them. Stepping off the train into the square gave her a panic attack. It had become familiar with time, but never comfortable.

She wondered if her mother had viewed her like that, another braying interruption in what would be an otherwise peaceful day. It was likely that her mother wouldn't even remember her. They hadn't allowed visits between them at all in the last few years of her living there. The worse, more terrible possibility was that her mother might have died without anyone mentioning it.

The train ride out of town took forever, nearly two hours, during which time she nervously tapped on the window and shifted in her seat. She couldn't think of a clever lie, so she simply stated her case. "I'd like to see my mother." She gave them the information they needed. It was the same receptionist that had always worked there, but the woman didn't recognize her.

Still, they acted like this sort of thing happened all the time. There was a short wait, but ultimately she was waved through. The guard didn't even wait on her. He just showed her the door and allowed her to go.

Her heart began to pound in her chest as she walked

in, stunned by how lucky she felt to be let through. The thunderous noise of her own excitement stopped dead the moment she saw the inside of her mother's room.

It was the same room that she'd always been in. It was all-white, white furniture and walls, no windows, with her mother positioned on the bed in the middle of the room. It was the same as it ever was, except her mother had changed. Instead of a beautiful woman reclined luxuriously while machines whirred all around her, she had become gray and tired. She was breathing laboriously, her hands draped almost lifelessly over her lap.

Her senses struggled to make sense of what was happening. There was something on the floor and the walls, something not white but grayish pink. She scanned it and scanned her mother, again and again, trying to understand. When it finally clicked, her stomach lurched.

It was her mother. Her mother had grown around the room. The crawling threads were her skin. She was turning the room into some kind of cocoon of her own flesh.

She burst into tears, retching, her body unable to choose whether sorrow or revulsion was its priority. She stepped slowly forward, the skin shifting and sliding under her shoes. Pieces of her mother fell from the ceiling with wet, slopping noises. She wept. She reached for her mother, but when her hand landed on her wrist, the skin began to slide, and she couldn't stop screaming.

The guard led her out, and somehow the staff all managed to push her to the train. The ride home was a blur, horrible and obscured, with her routinely bursting into ragged bouts of weeping despair. There were still bits of her mother stuck in the tread of her shoes, under her fingernails, in her hair. She rubbed her arms and face, but couldn't get the goo off.

She made it home very late, walked into her apartment, and closed the door behind her.

The worst thing wasn't that her mother might die, it was that she herself might live, through all the same trauma and horror, pinned to the bed and fed upon by children like little worms stuck to her belly, who she could no longer bring herself to see as her own. Who she no longer saw as children at all. The worst thing wasn't life or death, it was the potential she felt in her own body to become her mother. She touched her own skin, mortified by its elasticity. She rubbed it and rubbed it and when that didn't work she just began clawing at herself, scratching and bleeding and finally falling asleep.

She went to work that Wednesday the same as always and acted as though nothing had changed. The set-up was all the same, but when they told her it was time to start recording, she shook her head. "Actually, I've prepared something I'd like to read," she smiled, pushed the papers off to the side. There was a charged silence, but no voices came.

"I was thinking of last year when I saw a spider eat another spider, and why I couldn't forget it. It appeared to me and my dreams again and again. I couldn't understand why I was so interested in it. Obsessed, maybe. I watched TV all day and all night trying to forget, but it kept appearing in my mind."

She glanced upwards at the mirror. "It's because I viewed it as an analogy for my life." She smiled, triumphant to finally understand. "The point is, the more of myself I lost, the more we all become one. What is death, but a final and sudden erosion of our identities into nothingness?"

She paused. She had memorized the next line, but she still needed a moment to take a breath. "It's just that some basic truths still come as a shock. Nobody likes to think of it, but we've all started rotting well before we die."

The studio was silent. She lit a cigarette in the no-smoking studio and used it to burn the papers they had given her. She calmly reapplied her lipstick and waited for someone to come drag her to the final pit they would throw her in, whatever it might be.

Yet nothing happened. No one came. She waited and waited, but the voices never returned. After a while, the lights began to shut off. She eventually left, uncertain, and more afraid than she'd been before. The streets were emptying in the lateness of the day, and she was afraid she'd missed the bus, catching the last one only by seconds. The speakers were droning, as always.

When she made it home, she walked calmly down the dirty green carpeted halls, flanked by the faded yellow walls that made her feel so claustrophobic here. Her door was locked, and her key would no longer work. She tried for a while, then gave up, returning to the streets. It was dark, now. The streets, where she'd been warned again and again not to be caught out in at night, were empty. The bright blue lights of the police shone as they flashed down the alleys, but even with no one around, the speakers were still present. The voices loomed as ominously as the sky. It wasn't long before she heard her own voice, the voice that sounded just like her but said things she had never said. "I remember the last time I saw my mother, she told me she loved me...."

# SPRINGTIME

THE FIRST DAY OF SPRING, SHE SAID GOODBYE TO HER sister.

Ashley opened the door, and saw her sister laying on the ground, and knew she was gone. She began a wail that quickly wilted into a whimper. The room was destroyed. Furniture broken. Blood on the walls and floor. Her sister, smashed under careless feet like the crushed yellow blossoms that surrounded her. Dead.

Gone.

George Samson had been harassing them ever since their mother died. Ashley and Selena had changed the paths they took to town, put heavy curtains over the windows, grown hedges around the property. It didn't change anything. He kept creeping along the edges of their property, and people dismissed it, and now Selena was gone.

She began to clean the space. Picking up the broken glass, cleaning the blood from the walls, straightening her sister's legs out, covering her with a cloak. She swept and scooped and prepared, glancing nervously at the light outside. She needed the light to last.

She said a prayer for her sister. She sat at her feet and smoothed the blanket and brushed away her tears and tried to speak. The prayer was first, and then the spell. She chanted what their grandmother had taught them.

Selena's body began to shake. When Ashley asked the corpse of her sister who had killed her, Selena's blood poured from her pores and soaked through the blanket. She rasped his name dryly, yet there was still something of her sister's gentle lilt in the demonic growl that came from under the cloth, and it as that which made Ashley burst into tears.

Ashley knew who killed Selena, but the ritual mattered. She tied her sister to a sled and pulled her outside, not bothering to lock the door. There was nothing more valuable than Selena, and Selena was gone. Ashley would have to create an entirely different value system in order to continue on at all, but before any of that, she would have to take care of her sister's body.

As she began the long trip to the cemetery, the villagers she saw along the road looked away from her. Selena and Ashley's mother and aunts had once been respected healers. Now, Ashley was all that was left of them. She did not cry as she walked. She had wept all through the afternoon and had no tears left to give. She walked beyond the edge of town, and further still.

The cemetery appeared in the distance. Tombstones rose up against the horizon and loomed larger and larger until she was upon them. She crossed the first row of graves, then the next. Her feet moved methodically, one after the other, giving no trace of uncertainty. Even as she passed the last row, she continued to move. This would not be her sister's resting place. Her sister would not rest. She kept walking.

The sky began to fill with angry clouds, coming from all directions at once. She did not pull her cloak tighter or cover her hair; both whipped and snapped with the gusts. The wind grew cold, and she walked ahead in defiance of it. The trees swayed as far out as she could see on the horizon. The branches, with their newly forming buds, creaked overheard.

This was the walk of bones. Beyond the graveyard, into the hills. Skeletons littered the landscape, cracked and gray. Flowers grew up through the eye sockets of skulls, red and purple and white blossoms dotting a landscape of hard rock and sky. Life, clawing up through the cracks. Always clawing up.

The lake ahead raged. The oil-blue flame that covered its surface flickered wildly as she approached. Shadows grew and shrank and changed. Ashley kept moving until she reached the rocky bank of the pool of death and rebirth.

Finally, she lay her sister down, and gazed up at the dark, rolling clouds overhead. Lightning struck the water's surface again and again. Her heart raced. She knew that she could not stand long at the shore. Silhouettes of bizarre creatures twisted about just under the waves. She untied the cloak covering her sister and looked once more at her face.

Ashley smoothed Selena's eyebrow with her thumb and kissed her cheek, then covered her once more and shoved her into the lake.

The sled Selena was tied to immediately vanished

under the surface as if pulled with great force. The lightning worsened, and large drops of rain began to fall. Ashley yelled out the spell as she backed up as quickly as she could, hiding behind the rocks and trees that stuck up out of the bed of bones. A shrill scream rose from the lake, and a hand shot out of the water. Ashley began to shake violently, teeth chattering. The thing that was once Selena crawled its way out of the water.

Her skin was the same translucent blue of the flame. She walked painfully across the rocks, reaching for something far away. The footprints she left smoked and smoldered. Ashley sobbed to see her sister in pain, but she did not go to her. Selena walked intentionally back to the town, her body glowing with heat.

Ashley returned to the village only to retrieve her money and to listen to the screams as Selena worked her way through the village. Bones cracked and splintered in her hands. Blood washed over the town. Not just George. It hadn't been only George who had hurt her, but the whole town, ignoring the threat he posed.

Ashley listened, but she did not stop her brisk walk out of town. It was now the dead of night, and the path was dark and treacherous, but she knew she would have to keep moving. Selena was going to destroy everyone that ever did her harm, and that meant that she was going to make it to Ashley too someday.

# EXPLICIT

THE WEEKS LEADING UP TO HEATHER'S DEATH, I HAD
terrible dreams. Dreams where my deceased mother
dragged herself out of the ground to come to find me, her
bloody fingernails clawing down my face until I woke up
sobbing. Dreams where all the birds fell dead from the
sky, where children holding balloons full of blood and
bones flashed grins full of long, sharp teeth, where a man
whose arms could stretch and grow found me everywhere
that I would try to hide, his fingers reaching and cracking
and creeping towards me no matter how I ran. I'd started
sleeping on the couch to avoid waking my wife. She was
in no position to comfort me. She had other things to
worry about. She would be dead soon.

Heaven knows I'm not a saint, but above everything,
you have to understand that mine and Heather's last night
together isn't what I would have chosen. If she had to die,
there are more peaceful ways than being crushed and
rolled and shredded in a car, trying to scream through her
own blood as strangers watched her last horrific

moments. I would not have chosen to live carrying the burden of the knowledge of her death. I might be a monster, but I am not why Heather died.

I did not choose how we spent our last night together, but—in her way—Heather did choose her death. Looking back, you can see the threads of her life and how they all finally tied up. Every moment braided together like some nightmarish, sentient rope, squirming through time, wet and kinetic and writhing. Cosmic foreshadowing, which later became facts for me to recite to the police. "My name is Mary Kaye, the wife of the deceased Heather Kaye." Answering "yes, yes, yes," to all their questions in the hospital's lobby and refusing to cry. Absolutely refusing to cry.

With Heather gone, what was left? Just a widow and a will; and a pending investigation into my character and habits, and my wife ready to go in the ground forever. Just me, looking out the window as Heather's mother fell to her knees and screamed after experiencing the sight of her daughter's corpse, barely recognizable to her in death. She made that choice—it was her decision to look. Not mine.

I would not have chosen that for her. I would not have wished for her to spend the rest of her life haunted by the vision of her daughter's lifeless body. I refused to look. That was my choice, but it was taken away from me. I would see Heather again, and soon. Death changes some things, but it didn't change that.

Her mother attacked me there in the hospital, but I had taken the opiates that I found in my pocket, so I didn't react, just let her claw at me, shouting obscenities in my face. Heather's brothers pulled her off of me and comforted her. She cried and said she hated me, but I just stood there. I'm sure it sounds cold, but what could I have done?

I had bigger problems. I was tallying numbers. How many days can I stay in the house before her family claims it? How much cash do I have? Do I still have the backup credit card Heather gave me? Would I be sleeping in Heather's bed or on the streets?

"Forgive her," Heather's father whispered to me through his sobs. "She's in pain. Forgive her."

But forgiveness always comes easy to a woman like Heather's mother, and it's always been hard to come by for me. Whether I forgave her or not, the world would cradle and protect her so that she would always be surrounded by love even in her very ugliest moments, and nothing I could say or do would ever change that. She didn't need my forgiveness. Forgiving her would cost me a lot, but it wouldn't change who we are.

Anyway, forgive her for what? For the slap, or how they had failed Heather in her life so terribly that we all ended up standing in a hospital at four o'clock in the morning grieving her? For how they had left me flailing to clean up the wreckage left by their poor parenting decisions or for screaming in my face after my wife had died in my presence less than two hours prior? What could forgiveness even mean when Heather was dead on a cold table, no more than a short elevator ride away from where we stood?

Absently, I muttered, "It's nothing." I felt for my phone and house keys to ensure they were still there. The screen was smashed beyond repair, so I used the hospital phone to call a cab. I did not say "goodbye" to Heather's family. I wasn't worried about them. All they had to do was pray, and God would forgive them, but Heather will never forgive me.

I drank very little that night, so I remembered most of the events leading up to the accident. Heather had come home early from work, falling on the couch with a sigh, throwing her hands over her face. I sat down next to her and pulled her arm so she'd sit up. I massaged her shoulders. She pulled her shirt off, and we kissed for a long time, sitting on the couch together. There was a peacefulness to it, then she grabbed my wrists and bit me instead of kissing me, and things got sticky and hot between us until we were on the floor, and I was pulling her closer, as close as another person could be, and then closer still. Afterward, my tension was shattered for a while. It was temporarily blissful, in a hollow sort of way. It made me think of how things were before everything had become so painful between us.

We dressed, went to the premiere, and had dinner and drinks with her coworkers. When it was time to slow down, Heather sped up. I shrank into myself, no longer engaging, simply waiting to leave. We argued in the parking garage. I begged to drive, but she was stronger than me, even drunk, and I couldn't get the keys away from her. She threw me into a wall. I nearly got into a taxi instead. I got into the car at the last minute, closing my eyes and thinking of my mother, not listening to Heather. Thinking of the woman my mother had wanted me to be and how increasingly far away I felt from her.

So it was that I was in the car with Heather when she died, but I wasn't awake for it. I was knocked unconscious immediately. They said I'd crawled out of the car, but I don't remember that. To my recollection, when I awoke, it was in the ambulance. I had missed everything. I could see through the window that there was another ambulance following us. The EMTs made grim observations that no matter how quickly the second vehicle drove, it would never be fast enough, and I realized at that moment that Heather was gone.

I had some injuries; a concussion, cuts, bruises from the shattered glass, and scratches around my throat which they said had come from Heather. The thought of my wife clawing at my neck with her dying breaths sent chills through me. I pulled my jacket up over the scratches and shuddered.

I was relieved not to have died like Heather, with my insides crushed, laying on the side of the road twisted like a broken doll. Heather alive was different from Heather dead, yet they were the same, composed of the same molecules and everything. She had changed profoundly, with all the warmth gone, blue-lipped and broken, but with the same skin I'd dragged my lips down, the same eyes that watched me undress hundreds of times, and the hands that.

I could not look at her body. I refused to see.

Why I had survived, I would never understand. I think it might have been better for us all if she'd been the one who lived. As it was, we were finally free of one another. I was devastated.

I returned to the house on the hill where we'd lived for six years of our marriage. Rising above the other homes on the street, a white building with tall windows and a yard made of rocks, whose inside was as stark and modern as the outside and never looked very lived in at all. Even now, I refer to this as "Heather's house." She was the one that paid for it. At least, her family did. I never felt comfortable there. Sometimes I would return home from shopping, and her mother would be casually sitting in the living room. Such interruptions upset me. I hated vapid conversation in my own home. When I walked through my front door, I always wanted a blanket of silence to envelop me. When I brought it up to Heather, it caused an argument. She lived in terror of her parents, always afraid that they would take away her inheritance. They already withheld their love from her, and that seemed so much worse for some reason. Even when she no longer truly needed their money, she clung to it as the one thing they had given her.

My mother had lived and breathed for my happiness. The worst thing she'd done to me was to bring me into this godawful world, to begin with. And the worst thing I'd done to her was to hide the parts of me that she would not have been able to love. She suffered through bad jobs, a bad marriage, and chronic pain to give me a better life. I'd have given anything to keep her safe. To me, Heather's relationship with her parents seemed perverse.

I laid down on the couch and dreamed fitful dreams. Sitting on the bed with my mother, who asked me where my face was until I reached up and realized it was gone. Looking into the mirror, I saw a mess of blood and meat tissue where once I had lips and skin. Dreaming of Heather, pushing her fingers through my hair so gently only to turn her hand into a fist and pull me into a hard kiss as our flesh melted into a puddle at our feet.

Heather and I had met at a club on a chilly, damp night in November nearly eight years before, with rain in the air and ugly, distorted music growling from the bars. She walked up to me after I'd had a few drinks alone and started a conversation. She gave off an obnoxious mix of complete fragility and overwhelming arrogance that so many rich people have. Still, I'd been working in foodservice and was very interested in her nice clothes and casual indifference to spending money. She was pretty, too. Of course, she was. She was dressed in black, worn from late nights and skipped meals, looking like she already had one foot in the grave, but also soulful, with soft skin and troubled eyes. I let myself be drawn in. It always seemed like a mistake. Even then, I knew it was a mistake.

As we left the bar together, the streets were black and slick and wet with rain. The traffic lights lit our path from the bar to Heather's car, then to her hotel room. She didn't kiss me but instead pushed me onto the bed. She grabbed my thigh so hard it made me gasp, and I knew then and there that things would never be easy with her.

By the morning, I was drained, like I'd spent the night with a vampire. I ached and found bruises in various spots on my body throughout the day. I couldn't focus on anything. I resolved never to see her again, but a few hours later, when she texted me, "Where are you at?" I immediately responded, "Where do you want me?" I faked illness to leave work early, and after that, Heather and I were rarely apart.

Falling in love with Heather was a choice. She wasn't a good person, but I loved her. It was from my heart, but it was an economical choice, as well. It meant that I was able to give my sick mother better care. When I was working late hours every night to help pay for her hospitalization, I had fallen into a pit of self-hatred for not being able to care for her properly. I was desperate. Heather was my handsome devil, giving me the one thing I desired at the cost of something I could not afford to lose.

I didn't tell my mother about my relationship with Heather, just that she was a close friend. Even when we eloped, after moving my mother into hospice care in Heather's home, I let her think that Heather was simply a remarkably generous friend. Bedridden, my mother believed what she wanted to believe.

I suppose I could have felt guilty about lying to my mother, but I had always lied to her about women. There was never a good time, and I think it would have made it harder for her to love me. When she brought marriage up, I would shrug or politely lie. Knowing would have just made her feel like she had failed me as a mother, so what point would there be in that? It wasn't her fault, but she would have felt like it was. After all, she'd been the one that sent me off with my older cousin and her friends when I was a kid. One of them, Chris, took me out into the woods and shoved me against a tree and kissed me. Even back then, no one was gentle.

Chris threatened to beat me up if I told anyone about her kissing me, but I would never have told. I felt that I was in love with her, though I suppose that's not really what it was. For years, I believed that someday we would be married, but though Chris and I had a passionate affair that lasted many years, she eventually married a man named David when she was twenty-five, and I was twenty. We fought, and I wept, and she still married him, anyway. Now, I understand that it could not have gone any other way, but in that moment, I was shattered. Not so long after, I met Heather.

Ever since I was a girl, all I wanted was to take care of my mother, and I did it. Whatever else happened, it doesn't matter. After she was gone, I started taking pills, and I let all the darkness I'd been hiding take over for a while. That was about halfway through my marriage. I couldn't get out of bed at all.

That was when things went bad between Heather and me. She saw a side of me that she couldn't deal with, and that rejection of my innermost thoughts crushed me. If it had ever been right between us, it never was again after my mother died. Heather became more aggressive, more possessive, and I became more and more passive, letting the days drift by.

In the days after Heather's death, her family was angry at me, but I was more furious at them. It's not like it was the first time she drank too much and got behind the wheel. She had been out of control for months. Why hadn't they helped her? They'd always forced her to be so perfect. Trying to live up to their expectations made her a monster. For Heather's honor, I was furious with them.

For people like them, women like me don't mean a thing. Through their eyes, I was just there for Heather's money, at best a placeholder for some upper-class guy, but they never realized that I stayed after my mother died, and not for the money, either. I stayed because I was afraid for Heather. I was loyal to her, and I was angry with her, and I still wanted her. I still wanted her so much. Her family hated me, but they knew nothing of love. How could they? I suffered to be with Heather when they had only ever pushed her away.

Heather had at least made sure that I'd be taken care of. I was left to go over these documents with a fine-tooth comb alongside her lawyer, making sure I would get all the money owed to me by her estate. Again, her family was livid, and they called me a gold-digger and worse, but I couldn't bring myself to care. They may have lost a daughter, but they would die rich regardless of what Heather left for me. They were there for spite alone while I tried to find a way to live. I desperately needed to cover my bases. I'd have been out on the streets with nothing if they had their way. I never forgot that for a second as I spoke to them politely through my teeth in the presence of lawyers.

They hated that I was not grieving. They wanted me to be a wreck over Heather's death, but it would be wrong to say that I missed her. Not when she still felt so close. And I was so relieved that it had been only us in the accident, that no one else had been hurt, that if someone had to die, it was the person who put my life in danger that way. I was so happy that there would be no more arguments, that I could go anywhere and do whatever I wanted and not risk her ire. I was elated at never having to interact with her coworkers ever again. I was free but afraid, angry, and in mourning, all at once. I was overwhelmed with emotion, but her family wanted me to feel the one thing I couldn't feel – sorry. I refused to carry that burden alone. We had all failed her, but the only person Heather failed was me.

At Heather's funeral, I read a prepared speech. Of course, Heather's family was exhaustingly religious and would want me to thank God for the love of Heather. A love that had been scraping like broken glass over the bloody surface of my heart since the day we met. Rather than thank God for that, I could kill him and love it.

God protects them, but I did everything I could to protect my mother, and she was still dead in the ground before her time. I refused to be a martyr—if I could trade every one of their lives to bring my mother back, I would. Morality is meaningless in the face of death. In the end, their god is money, comfort, and leisure, and nothing more.

I walked calmly to the podium and began, "Heather, every day without you is a new lesson in heartache..." My words tumbled forward, cracking from the genuine pain of losing her but laced with anger older than the loss. I stumbled and staggered through, and Heather's family seemed to soften as I spoke, even if I continued to harden to them. I avoided looking at the coffin that held Heather's body. In the end, I concluded, "I know that we'll be reunited someday in Heaven, my love," but I left the stage thinking after they close the lid of that coffin, Heather, I'll never see your face again. This time is the last.

The next few weeks moved at a snail's pace. I had meeting after meeting with investigators from all sides of the situation that were trying to understand how I got away from the accident relatively unscathed. They would note, "it's a miracle you survived."

"A miracle," I would agree.

In the end, there is just no way to fake an accident like that. I couldn't have planned it. Heather's family began to believe that they had overreacted, and they started to treat me more kindly. I, for my part, hated them—more clearly, with more definition, than ever before. I was getting tired of it all. The longer it went on, the more I wanted to jump off a cliff right into the ocean. I might have done it if I didn't feel so sure that Heather would be there at the bottom. Waiting for me.

I'd been going out just to avoid going home. Drinking too much. Spiraling. I was at a private club Heather used to bring me to, wearing a black wig and a purple mask for the superhero theme of the night. I was surprised to run into Heather's sister Helena, dressed exactly like Heather. Black jeans, black button-up shirt with several buttons undone, no bra, short socks, some jewelry, beautiful, expensive black shoes. A theme night of a different kind: dress up as my dead wife. Both of us played pretend. Still somehow searching for Heather in the crowd.

She approached me the same way Heather had that first night, openly flirting and spending money to impress me. I started to gather my things to leave, hoping against hope that I could have the strength to walk away from this perverse scenario, but on my way back from the bathroom, Helena intercepted me. As others danced around us, she kissed me, and as if all my concerns meant nothing, I was pulling her close to me, letting her run a hand over my lower stomach, brushing her fingers past the hem of my skirt, and pushing her hand inside me.

On some level, the part of me that was my mother's daughter was appalled. But it was the equally undeniable part of me that just wanted everything to burn that let her take me home.

Helena was kissing my neck, but I kept seeing Heather. At one point, she was standing behind her sister, glaring at me, and later, it was Heather after the accident, bleeding and broken, whose breath was hot against my skin. I pulled Helena closer to me and gasped when she bit my neck. Her fingers pressed just a little too hard into my skin, and we pulled each other's clothes off and fell into bed. I thought I could still see Heather, so I closed my eyes as I touched Helena all over and moaned to encourage her to touch me back. Maybe Heather would see this after all, and she'd stop haunting me and start haunting her sister instead. Maybe she had already started. When I awoke, Helena was gone.

I know it was ghoulish. The whole scenario a terrible fairy tale, ominous and full of double meanings. A fantasy that had become corrupted and would not release me.

The next time we ran into each other, Helena walked up behind me and put her hands over my eyes. "Guess who?" she said.

I held her wrists where they were just for a moment, welcoming the darkness her hands brought, shutting my eyes as tight as I could, and trying to pretend. I tried to pretend that this was anyone else in the world but who it was.

We kissed in the dirty, vibrating, black-walled room. It was so hot and humid, like the night when Heather and I had met, and it all faded into a hazy dream. She followed me home, walking not beside me but half a block behind me. Stalking me like a cat. I remember her skin sliding over me as if it had crawled from her flesh and was all that was left of her. Human-shaped, but nothing inside, only a soft, amorphous hide. No eyes, only holes where eyes would have been. I saw and felt and touched wet skin and nothing else, and it filled my mouth, pressed down against me, pushed inside of me, and covered me completely as I shook and moaned.

When I woke up, gray sunlight filtered through the tinted window over my bed, beating into my eyelids until

I finally gave in and got up. I was still drunk, but in that half-sober way, that makes you remember every mistake you ever made in your life. Vague memories tugged at me. Helena had come home with me, but who knows where she'd gone. Maybe her skin had followed the rest of her home. Maybe that could be the end of this.

Of course, I had realized by then that it wasn't Helena I had been sleeping with. Helena was in Berlin, doing whatever the children of wealthy parents do when they say they're "studying abroad." She'd been dating one of the guys from some annoying band for half a decade. An affair with Helena would have been sordid enough, but this was even worse. The marks on my thigh made me realize the truth. Everything had been a blur, but the marks were the same, the same ones I'd had the night after I met Heather. Bites that left small bruises over my thighs. I was sleeping with Heather, or Heather's ghost, or maybe a demon in the shape of Heather, but definitely somehow Heather. I tried to remember more details, but everything was such a blur from the last few weeks. I was crumbling.

I pulled the wig off, but I left the mask on. I turned the water on to take another bath, but it came out brown and orange, so I shut it off and lay on the tile floor instead. Crying, I thought of Heather.

That night, I had a dream.

I was walking through a soundless field. It was a perfect summer day—green grass, blue sky, flowers—but there was no noise. This is how I might have known it was a dream, but it wasn't any more surreal than life had been for the past weeks. Everything so real and foreboding, the veil between reality and fantasy so thin that I could poke my hand to the other side. I wandered for a long time, crossing broken-down wooden fences, and losing all sense of direction.

I came upon a small pond shrouded by a gathering of dead trees. The shadows of their gray limbs stretched across the moss-coated surface of the murky water. I stared into the pool's center, where it seemed like there was nothing but a void. The surface of the water rippled. The air caught in my throat.

Was there something? Something in the water? Shadows danced over the pool, and my eyes flitted around, trying to see. A mass began to rise. I staggered backward.

A human head. A body began to surface, stretching its hands up in the air.

Heather. I choked and covered my hand with my mouth. She was naked and now standing waist-deep in the pond. Patches of the moss clung to her, dripping. Parts of her had been eaten, but only a little. There were patches of missing skin, and her eyes gone from their sockets, but my heart raced to see her nonetheless.

The memories I had denied began to rise once more. I remembered that last moment in the car when Heather had turned the wheel sharply, purposefully, and we'd crashed into the median. In her last moments on earth, she ripped at my skin with all the energy she had and tried to take me with her. Here, looking where her eyes would be, I remembered her in my skin. I remembered walking around late at night, creeping through the streets, my body not mine but Heather's, causing massive gaps in my memory. I remembered my own hands rushing over my body, Heather delighting in the sensation of me.

A piercing, echoing cry, Heather screamed, and I buckled under the noise. Finally, it began to ebb, and I staggered, slipped, and fell into the water. I reached for her, water sloshing around me. Slime clung to my skin and seemed to sink into my bones. Sweat trickled down my face, mixing with the oily pool.

I kissed Heather. Her cold lips and thick tongue pressed against mine, slick and rotten. I'd been trapped in the dreamlike haze since her death lifted, and everything seemed clearer than ever. I gasped for air once and was pulled under the pond's surface by the cold hands of people I could not see. Dozens of slimy, boney fingers grabbed my legs and dragged me down. I screamed, and the air vanished from my lungs. The last thing I saw was the sunlight as it sparkled through the black pond and Heather's brackish, empty eye sockets.

When I woke up, drenched in putrid water, in Heather's bed, I kicked and jerked and screamed with Heather's hands around my neck. I fell backward off the bed, crashed to the floor, and ran downstairs. I paced the kitchen, holding my phone, and called Heather's mother.

"Hello?" she answered after a couple of rings. When I didn't immediately speak, she said, "Mary?"

As I panted into the phone, I realized that Heather's mother was not and could not be my mother. My mother was lost to me forever. I could never call her again. She was in Heaven, where we could never meet. One place where I could never, ever go. My mother was gone forever, while Heather hung over me and slipped inside of me whenever she wanted.

I hung up and threw my phone across the kitchen. I ran up the stairs, where I found Heather, covered in blood like she had been the night of the accident, staring back at me. She touched her collarbone, and I touched mine. She unbuttoned her shirt, and I unbuttoned mine. She pulled off her clothes and held her palm towards me. I staggered forward, pressed my hand against hers, then pulled it down and placed it against my hip. I closed my eyes and sighed softly as her hand began to move.

When I woke up, I was lying on the floor. I slowly reached up and pulled the mask from the club back over my face, leaving it there.

That night, I sat on the floor, I stared at the wall, I looked at the sky, and tried to see stars that were no longer there. Trying to see on a molecular level. Trying to see the atoms in the air. The room pulsed around me. I drank, and worried, and cried for my old life and everything that might have been.

Late into the night, Heather watched me from the corner of the room, saying nothing at all. I stood up out of bed, and I walked into her. She did not stagger; she only merged with me, wrapping around my body and pulling me inside. The mirror on the wall would not show my reflection. Whoever I was before, the woman my mother wanted her daughter to be, I know she's gone now.

I'll never see her face again. That time was the last.

# THE LITTLE THINGS
# THAT COME AND GO

I WOKE UP THIS MORNING TO A BRANCH SCRATCHING MY
window. I complained to my landlord that the branches
needed to be cut, and they have been. A woman has come
and cut them. Many times now. The branches were here
yesterday morning, gone by the afternoon, and back again
by 5:00 a.m. when the sky was still gray and black and the
streets were full of fog. The branches came back, just like
the cat, the broken glass in my backyard, and the graffiti
that says "The Devil" in thick white letters on the wall
behind my house. I can't get rid of anything anymore. I
throw it out. I take the cat to the shelter, I clean up the
debris, I cut down the branch. I do it all again, and again,
and again. It just keeps coming back.

The worst of all the things that won't go away is the
body of the woman that died. I found her in the backyard
not long after I moved in. She had crawled through the
fence and passed away in the backyard in the early hours
of the morning one unlucky Sunday. She was the first
thing that was taken away from here, in an ambulance,

pronounced dead. No ID. No one claimed the body. Nameless.

Weeks later, I visited her grave. It was marked by a small stake with a number on it. It might not have even been hers. There's nothing to say it was other than the man on the other side of the phone when I called to check, so he could have said any of them and I'd have believed that it was the same woman. I stood there awkwardly, listening to a random YouTube video of a priest delivering last rites for a woman named Marguerite Stanton who had died of the Coronavirus and pretending it was a proper funeral and she was surrounded by loved ones, not just one lonely girl with headphones on standing in a cemetery in the middle of the day, playing pretend.

The prayers were long and rambling. He prayed for her to find peace, but I don't believe she found peace. I don't know if any of us do. When I came home, she was in the backyard again. I covered her with branches, but they were back on the tree by the morning. She's there again today, lying rotten among the fallen tree branches. Her mouth is eaten away by the ants. They have covered her, and the trees, and the dirt, and there are more of them every day.

The woman speaks to me from her empty eye sockets. She says, "We could trade places and you'd never even notice." Or maybe I misheard her. Maybe she didn't say anything at all. Maybe it's just the buzz of the ants. But I think that's what she said.

The sanitation workers come every Wednesday to pick up the trash that will be back in the basket in the back-yard by Thursday morning. Even if just for a day, I wish they would take the woman, and everything else, along with them. I wish they could take me, far from here. Trash is piling up in the yard. I asked my neighbor about it, but he was so clearly confused that I had to cut the conversation short and go back inside. He had no idea what I was talking about. None of the other houses are affected, and it brings bad energy to try and discuss it with them at all. Now, he hesitates before he says "hello."

The branches scrape against the side of the house all day and all night. The old woman whispers to me from somewhere deep inside my mind even after the ants have eaten much of her throat away.

The ants stay at the edge of the porch. They never come into the house, but the backyard is covered by them. They slowly ate the trees alive, leaving rotting husks, falling apart on my balcony and over the roof. I can't set foot out there anymore. The ants crawl up my legs and it makes me cry. I had to jump in a scalding hot shower to wash them off, and I could feel them biting me as I did. I was covered in tiny red bumps after that, red bumps that go away, and then come back, go away, and then come back.

I can never get rid of the ants. Even when the woman is gone, they are still there. Later, I saw them climbing back up the drain, scraping and clicking and crawling. I had to take each and every one of them back outside, and even now I can hear them.

When did it start?

I moved here a couple months ago. I needed a cheaper, bigger place to live, so I left the city to a place I could afford. Everything was fine in the beginning. I was haunted by nightmares, but that isn't abnormal. The house was always very cold, but it was winter. I felt alone, but that's what I was. There was a certain fact-based truth behind my night terrors that made them feel reasonable. Traumatic childhood, unstable adulthood, night terrors. A series of built-in starts and stops. A simple but non-negotiable connect-the-dots puzzle that made up my present situation.

The house was bigger than any I'd lived in before, and empty. I didn't have money for furniture, so I sat on the floor and slept on a mattress that had been left upstairs. Every step I made through the halls echoed and creaked. I, already quiet as a mouse, tried to be even quieter still. I didn't want to disturb the place. It always felt like I was intruding on something, someone, who had been there all along. Since before my time. There was a family in the house before me, and they had left a sense of ownership over the premises that always gave me the inclination that I was trespassing. Not that they were haunting me, just that the house would never be mine the way that it was once theirs. I felt confined to my room at night and would walk the halls only in the morning, breathing the heavy air.

It was the first week of my time there that the woman died in the backyard, and shortly thereafter that the ants began to arrive. I found her in the morning. She was propped up against the wall, not moving, not breathing. I stared at her, open-mouthed, for many minutes before I finally called 911. It took them hours to arrive. In the meantime, I agonized over what to do. It seemed wrong not to cover her up, but if she'd been murdered, doing so would disturb the scene of the crime. I stayed back, staring at her through the window. She wore a skirt and jacket, and a gold necklace. Her nails were painted red, and she had long brown hair. I would guess she was around fifty. Of all the people you might find dead in your backyard, she seemed particularly strange. It looked like she'd just come from work.

I stood there, imagining all the different possibilities and scenarios that might have led her to me as I waited for the authorities to arrive and take her away. Was she murdered? Did she overdose? Did her body simply fail her? Was it a new kind of plague?

The police eventually arrived and did everything I suspected they would, which is more or less nothing. They said that it seemed she'd simply died of heart failure, or some other terrifyingly random, instantaneous, trace-less death that any one of us could experience at any moment. I couldn't stop thinking of a heart stopping, just like a watch.

Why had she chosen my yard, of all the yards? Of all the nearby houses, mine was the only one with a tall chain link fence surrounding the property. Why go to the extra effort to climb through? They couldn't say. Days passed, and weeks, and still nobody knew who she was. Finally, she was buried, one among many in a small sea of white stakes jutting out of the ground.

I couldn't get the woman out of my mind. She kept coming into my thoughts. I paced up and down the stairs, unable to understand why she'd come into my life in such an arbitrary, ugly way. I thought of her unblinking eyes. When I looked back outside at the now empty space where she was found, surrounded by police tape that I would tear down again and again and again, I was sure I was hallucinating. For the first time, the words appeared on the slowly collapsing brick wall in the back of my property, one that had once belonged to a garage that no longer stood. "The Devil." Written in great, large letters in dripping white spray paint on the brick wall behind my house where the woman in the smart red suit had breathed her last.

That was also the day I found the cat in the walls. I had never heard it before, but there was suddenly a sharp wailing that followed me throughout the house. Jarred as I was by the discovery of the woman, I thought it must be her ghost. Only when I knocked a little hole in the wall and saw a yellow eye staring back out did I realize—it was a cat. The screams had sounded so remarkably human.

The cat was feral, and it was obvious immediately that I couldn't keep her. I opened the door and waited for her to leave, but instead, she hunted me through the house, diving at me and clawing me. I had never been very close with animals, but none had reacted to me like this before. I finally managed to get her into a box, and drove her to the shelter. I agreed to pay for getting her fixed and giving her shots and assumed they'd adopt her out as a working cat. However, when we made it to the vet, she purred and rubbed against his hands. Suddenly, she seemed domestic. She stared at me without emotion as I edged awkwardly back out through the front door of the vet's office, intending never to see the cat again.

In the night, I woke up with the cat's eyes staring at me, and I screamed. I leapt up, and the cat jumped too, ripping my arm with her claws. I wanted to believe that it was a different cat, but it was clearly the one from before, with the same small diamond-shaped patch of white fur at the center of her throat. Blood covered my arm and it made a terrible mess on the bathroom sink. Too tired to clean it up, I almost left it for the morning until I saw the cat lapping at it. I retched and turned on the faucet and scared the cat away. I cleaned up every drop. When I finally walked back towards my bed, I saw the woman out of my window.

She was in exactly the same position she'd been in when I found her. Her arms limp, but open, as if waiting to embrace me.

I only called the police once more, complaining of the graffiti and the woman. When they arrived, both were gone, and I had to pretend to pay attention while the cops looked at me like I was hysterical. I stayed silent and nodded, smiling optimistically when they started to close their rambling monologues. "Thank you. Thank you so much," I said, and shut the door on them as quickly as I could. I trotted back to the window looking out over the backyard. The woman wasn't there, but the graffiti was.

"The Devil."

Over this short amount of time, the woman's eyes, throat, and parts of her hands have all rotted or been eaten away, and her dress has grown dirtier. When the ants don't feed on her, the crows do, diving and whipping about in the wind with abandon, her fingers and toes breaking off and vanishing into their beaks as they fly away. They'll be back tomorrow. Everything always back tomorrow.

I've stopped taking calls from friends. They didn't understand me before, and I can't imagine that they would now. In some strange way, I feel a tenuous thread between us has snapped and I've been put adrift. My eyes are blue but they've become gray with weariness and there are always red circles around them. I feel that you can tell my age by counting the circles around my eyes like the rings inside a tree.

When I first arrived here, I pulled a board out of a basement window and discovered a giant spider sprawled across its web between the glass and the board. I didn't know spiders could be so big. I stared at it for a long time and chose to leave her be. Yesterday, I walked up to the window once more, and again I pried the board away.

The spider was still there, bristling hairs and spindly legs, and a back that looked like a great green eye, flecked with yellow and gold. The ants were eating her alive. I wanted to knock them off of her, but there were too many, and they'd eaten so much. As she curled up, I saw my reflection in her eyes. I put the board back up, and my knees gave way, and I cried. She might as well have been the last friend I had.

Sleep that night was impossible. I was in a cold sweat, and every time I would start to doze off, I would feel insects crawling on me. I dreamed that the old woman was in the room with me, a low, angry hiss coming from what was once her eyes. The cat glowered at me, too tired to attack. I shook and thrashed and clawed at my arms.

I saw ants inside today. Only a few, climbing in through the front door. I stopped cold, my heart thudding and the strange constant static of their thoughts rising in my ears. I stepped backward, but they were on the other side of the house, too. I guess that's when I knew that this was all going to end. There's no way out. They'll come inside, now. Their slow movement is methodical and winding. There will be no escaping them.

I look out the window, and the backyard is full of big

black beetles. The ants are swarming and devouring them. I watch beetle legs vanishing into clipping little mouths, and I wonder what it will feel like when it's me. The dying noise of the spider won't leave my ears.

The woman is sitting with her back against the brick wall, with "The Devil" in chalk vanishing and reappearing in flashes above her head. Maybe she accidentally let her soul slip away and left her body behind, and something else crawled in to take its place. The woman has been smiling and making an ugly noise with what remains of her throat for hours.

When this began, I believed it was all a mistake. It seemed so sudden and random. I was sure things would go back to normal soon, whatever that even meant for someone like me. Now, the loose threads slowly braid together, and I see that the ants had begun marching my way a long, long time ago. Every step led us here. People are like that, too. People are eaten alive by their own pathos. People are like ants, too. They swarm and devour, just like ants do.

I back slowly away from the window, into the darkness of the room, and I listen to the crunching exoskeletons and the soft rip of the gooey flesh underneath.

The light blinks on, and off, and on, and off. I stare at myself in the mirror as my face goes from light to shadows to light to shadows. The steady clicking of the switch flipping up and down sounds like it's coming from a hundred feet away. I click it down one last time. I stare at my face in the mirror, in the dark.

It takes me a long time to remember what I am. When I do, I'm in the backyard, slumped against the wall, ants crawling inside my throat. It's shocking, and I retreat back into the past, back when I had a body that was alive and whole. I spent hours gasping and retching into the bloody bathroom sink.

I spend the night wrapped in a blanket, listening to the ants. They want me to return to the body that they were eating so they can finish their meal, but I know that I can't manage to go out again today. I'll go back out tomorrow when I have something more to give.

# Afterword

Thank you for reading my story collection. We were in the weeds for a while there but we've come through on the other side. As nearly all of these stories deal with queer characters behaving badly at varying degrees, I have some notes on the things that inspired each of them. Looking back, so many of these characters fit the mold of classic queer villains of yesteryear, which is, as someone born in the mid-80s, much of what I was raised on. I hope I at least gave them some nuance before sending them to their ultimately still quite tragic fates. While I resist moralization of these tales due to their ambiguous personal nature, I don't mind if you find some for yourself. After all, these are your stories, now.

**Slipping But Not Falling** - When it came time for QueerSpec's fiction anthology *Decoded Pride* to release its second year, I had been preoccupied with the image of a beautiful fat blonde woman in a wide-brimmed hat lurking around a hotel during a storm, which transformed into a number of story possibilities (this character "Sasha" appears in my narrative horror podcast, "Tales From The Sapphire Bay Hotel"). I loved the idea of a morally-ambiguous villain whose evils are more naturalistic; she is only trying to feed her family, in this case, her lover, who just so happens to be a sea monster. Utilizing her as a side character made it possible to focus on the story of Jessica, a woman who is leaving a toxic relationship. Having gone on long road trips alone during chaotic and uncertain times in my life, there is something autobiographical in her journey, popping in at places that aren't necessarily welcoming to outsiders.

**The Last Days of the Plague** - I don't think it's an exaggeration to say that the COVID-19 pandemic broke a lot of our brains. As I've more or less accepted that I'll be masking for the rest of my life, I spent a lot of time considering how we could easily have gone extinct due to the lack of hygienic practices during the "main event" years of the bubonic plague. I think a lot about how during that time, people believed that God was striking humanity down for its sins and it seemed that all would perish in the end. Though we now know that the people of Europe ultimately survived, the statistics of just how many lives were lost and the cultural ramifications are stunning. It made me consider what it would be like to be surrounded by dead bodies and filth, truly believing you were experiencing the end times.

**The Hollow Bones** - This story underwent several changes, first showing a much more violent end for many of the birds in the story until I realized that they were the unspoken heroes and deserved a much more dignified context. It began with a friend mentioning that he knew a couple with some similarities to the bird-lovers in this tale, and I couldn't get the image of a toxic relationship going rapidly downhill in a house filled with expensive birds out of my head. I love Cin, who is not the POV character and is seen mostly in a disparaging light by her ex, and I love that they are both classic fairy tale style villains, with Cin embodying a "witch in the woods" vibe while our protagonist ultimately walks away as an "enigmatic city-dwelling occultist." Many of the stories in this collection occur kind of off to the side of a horror film, meaning this is a horror film told by one of the supporting characters who was not there when the murders or the monstrous transformations occurred and only saw the fallout from these events.

**The Death of a Drop of Water** - I have notoriously devastating period cramps so this was a bit based on that experience of having something that leaves you bedridden that many people don't see as an issue. Likewise, stories of people (especially women) being left by their spouses while suffering extreme illness are concerningly common. A now-deceased friend went through a similarly-motivated divorce, and even just scratching the surface of that scenario as a bystander felt like a horror story in itself. I would have loved for this character to have had a happier ending, and I hope that she ultimately found a way to make the bizarre backward reality work for her because she really didn't deserve all that.

**A Small Light** - After I watched "What Keeps You Alive," I was particularly affected by the narrative of two queer women off in the woods to celebrate their honeymoon only for one to turn on the other and go to absurd means to try and kill her. I loved that movie, but for my own peace of mind, I was determined to write a story in which a similar married couple had a happy ending, however, it was impossible. As I introduced the two women at the heart of "A Small Light," I sympathized with each of them and respected their love so much, but the conclusion insisted on being significantly more ambiguous than I wanted it to be. I might not gravitate toward happy endings overall, but this story is proof that I tried, but the characters and the circumstances just wouldn't go for it.

**Red Lips in a Blue Light** - When I saw the submission portal for *The New Flesh*, I was immediately excited about the idea of an anthology based on the works of David Cronenberg. *The Brood* and *Videodrome* are two of my favorite films despite both being mostly unpleasant to watch, and there's something about the TV gloss turned body horror vibes of his work that always compels me. The central character is lost from beginning to end, and her vibe reminds me a bit of Winston Smith in 1984, who attempts to rebel against the system only to be crushed by it. Maybe she finds a supportive community of her siblings living in the tunnels like Morlocks and they find peace together. I wish her luck.

**Springtime** - This was inspired by the imagery of a vengeful, demonic woman, impossible to reason with, raining terror on the countryside. Neither she nor the person that summons her has any control over her, she'll keep doing what she was raised to do until it's done. Likewise, it is inspired by the difficult choices we're forced to make after the death of a loved one, though often not quite so extreme as the choices made by this character. In the end, everything from the funeral to the mourning process is about us rather than them because what they would have wanted becomes a sort of amorphous thing; they can no longer speak for themselves.

**Explicit** - I love this protagonist because she is probably on-paper the shittiest person in the book. I wanted her to be a study of someone whose options are severely limited due to her sexuality and class, who sees society as a legitimately evil thing, but who never seems to hate the people that have done her the most harm. She never goes too far into details about her relationship with her mother, who she paints as saintlike but the seeds of her self-loathing are very much in that dynamic. I think if she tried to describe it to a therapist, they would view it as abusive, but we're seeing someone who is committed to maintaining the idea that her mother was perfect. Likewise, Heather is an abusive alcoholic, but our "hero" never seems to hate her, but she does hate her family for living in a fantasy world. I just loved this person for doing so much work to defend the worst people in her life and finding herself unable to understand what a healthy relationship dynamic could even look like.

**The Little Things That Come and Go** - This is one of the first short stories I ever wrote, and it has been rejected by just about every horror anthology in existence. Yet, much in line with the story itself, I've never quite been able to let it go. Several elements are taken directly from one of the most emotionally painful and disappointing times of my adult life. I had moved to a place looking for a fresh start only to see old problems coming back on me tenfold until I had to leave the city entirely. I reworked my life into something more sustainable with the support of long-time friends, but this character is very much an embodiment of my emotional state while I was still in the thick of things, problems and memories she thinks she has moved past returning and piling up around her as she finds herself caught in an unworkable situation. For me, the only solution was to leave, but for this character, she can't, and it crushes her.

# Previous Appearances

- A Small Light - *Decoded Pride* by QueerSpec
- The Last Days of the Plague - *Pandemic Unleashed* by Skywatcher Press
- The Hollow Bones - *Decoded Prise* by QueerSpec
- The Death of a Drop of Water - *The Fiends in the Furrows 2* by Nosetouch Press
- A Small Light - The No Sleep Podcast by Creative Reasoning
- Red Lips in a Blue Light - *The New Flesh* by Weirdpunk Books
- Explicit - *Pluto in Furs 2* by Plutonian Press

# About the Author

Sara Century got her start as a writer through the magical world of music zines. Though she would likely die from embarrassment to read one of those early pieces today, it led to a lifetime of work ranging from horror stories to narrative podcasts to feminist criticism to personal essays and beyond. Her best known zine remains "How to Become a Lesbian Vampire Movie," a comedic overview on the importance of lesbian vampires to queer culture. She has had her horror fiction spotlighted in anthologies like The No Sleep Podcast, performed countless live readings, saw her personal essays printed through sites like Bandcamp and The Gutter Review, worked through several websites from SYFY to Adweek, started some podcasts, speculative fiction anthologies, and publishing companies, and adopted some rabbits and cats which live together in harmony with the combined mission of running under her legs when she tries to make coffee in the morning.

*Grief Rituals* - Sam Richard

From Wonderland Award-Winning author Sam Richard comes twelve more uncomfortable tales of sorrow, ruination, and transformation.

A young widow joins a spousal loss support group with bizarre methods of healing. An aging punk is stalked by something ancient and familiar in the labyrinthian halls of an art complex. A couple renting out a small movie theater are interrupted by a corrosive force of nature. Through these stories of weird horror and visceral sorrow, Richard shows us ways grief can be transcendent—but only if we know which rituals to practice.

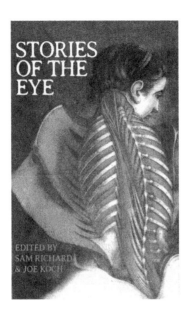

*Stories of the Eye* edited by Sam Richard & Joe Koch

An anthology of horror stories exploring the relationships between artists and their subjects. Featuring stories from Andrew Wilmot, M. Lopes da Silva, Gwendolyn Kiste, Hailey Piper, Roland Blackburn, Ira Rat, Donyae Coles, Matt Neil Hill, Brendan Vidito, LC von Hessen, Gary J. Shipley, and editors Joe Koch and Sam Richard. *Stories of the Eye* violently explores the connection of art to the body, the cosmos, madness, depression, grief, trauma, and so much more.

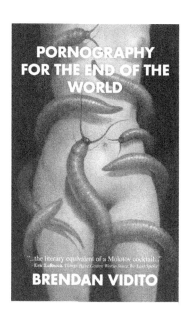

*Pornography for the End of the World* - Brendan Vidito

The end of the world demands a new form of pornography . . .

From Brendan Vidito, the Wonderland-Award-winning author of *Nightmares in Ecstasy*, comes nine tales of apocalyptic body horror. A young man is initiated into a cult that worships sickness and disease. Survivors of a nuclear holocaust make a pilgrimage to the last movie theater in existence. Premonitions of disaster haunt a loving couple doomed to watch each other die. Each story pulsates with Vidito's characteristic dark humor, atmospheric tension, and visceral prose. This is pornography for the devotee of horror, the morbidly curious—pornography for the end of the world.

" . . . the literary equivalent of a Molotov cocktail . . . "

— ERIC LAROCCA (*THINGS HAVE GOTTEN WORSE SINCE WE LAST SPOKE*)

# WEIRDPUNK
# STATEMENT

*Thank you for picking up this Weirdpunk book!*
*We're a small press out of Minneapolis, MN and our goal is to*
*publish interesting and unique titles in all varieties of weird*
*horror and splatterpunk, often from queer writers (though not*
*exclusively). It is our hope that if you like one of our releases,*
*you will like the others.*
*If you enjoyed this book, please check out what else we have to*
*offer, drop a review, and tell your friends about us.*
*Buying directly from us is the best way to support what we do.*
*www.weirdpunkbooks.com*